T0198922

A Tattooed Palm

A Novel

Naomi L. Carter

WESTBOW
P R E S S®
A DIVISION OF THOMAS NELSON
& ZONDERVAN

Copyright © 2020 Naomi L. Carter.

All rights reserved. No part of this book may be used or reproduced by any means, graphic, electronic, or mechanical, including photocopying, recording, taping or by any information storage retrieval system without the written permission of the author except in the case of brief quotations embodied in critical articles and reviews.

This is a work of fiction. All of the characters, names, incidents, organizations, and dialogue in this novel are either the products of the author's imagination or are used fictitiously.

WestBow Press books may be ordered through booksellers or by contacting:

WestBow Press
A Division of Thomas Nelson & Zondervan
1663 Liberty Drive
Bloomington, IN 47403
www.westbowpress.com
1 (866) 928-1240

Because of the dynamic nature of the Internet, any web addresses or links contained in this book may have changed since publication and may no longer be valid. The views expressed in this work are solely those of the author and do not necessarily reflect the views of the publisher, and the publisher hereby disclaims any responsibility for them.

Any people depicted in stock imagery provided by Getty Images are models, and such images are being used for illustrative purposes only. Certain stock imagery © Getty Images.

Unless otherwise cited, scripture is quoted from the King James Version of the Bible.

Scripture quotations marked (NIV) are taken from the Holy Bible, New International Version®, NIV®. Copyright © 1973, 1978, 1984, 2011 by Biblica, Inc.™ Used by permission of Zondervan. All rights reserved worldwide. www.zondervan.com The "NIV" and "New International Version" are trademarks registered in the United States Patent and Trademark Office by Biblica, Inc.™

ISBN: 978-1-9736-8336-0 (sc)
ISBN: 978-1-9736-8338-4 (hc)
ISBN: 978-1-9736-8337-7 (e)

Library of Congress Control Number: 2020900348

Print information available on the last page.

WestBow Press rev. date: 1/13/2020

First, to the Lord Jesus Christ, who saved me and preserved me to this hour. Then to family and friends who have believed in me and my calling all these years.

Acknowledgments

As always, I thank my God for sending Jack Carter back to me. His love for me and belief in me is essential every day.

Thanks to my first readers for the valuable insights, comments, and suggestions. Any mistakes in this work are the author's responsibility.

Finally, my profound appreciation to our neighbors who supported Jack and me through the twenty-four days following my recent back surgery, until I was able to drive again. And kudos to the doctors, nurses, and staff of the hospital and rehabilitation facility for their top-notch care, enabling a good recovery in just four months.

Thank you also to the staff at WestBow Press for bringing this work to completion.

Can a woman forget her suckling child, that she should not have compassion on the son of her womb? Yea, they may forget, yet will I not forget thee. Behold I have graven [tattooed] thee upon the palms of my hands.

—*Isaiah 49:15–16 (KJV)*

Chapter 1

Aims Wallace's eyes were drawn to Rick Holt, who was in the copilot's seat, talking on his cell phone. She saw the contingency response office drop away and recede as she put the Osprey hybrid aircraft into full horizontal flight and turned to a southwest heading.

Aims squirmed in the pilot's seat, trying to find a comfortable fit. But too many other fannies had tried to do the same thing, so the thinly padded chair didn't have much comfort left to offer. In fact, this aircraft offered few amenities for anyone because passenger transport wasn't part of its job description.

Off to the east, the midnight blue was softening to hues of pink, peach, and coral as the rising sun began to burn off the haze and turn the sky from cobalt to shades of azure. Her call to duty had been cryptic. She was just told to file a flight plan for Marco Island Executive Airport. The charts showed the airport was nestled against the side of Naples, Florida. What was the navy doing down there that she, Rick, and Larry Robb needed to investigate? Hopefully, that was what Rick was finding out on his phone call. But when he ended the call, he just sat staring out the cockpit window. Whatever it was, it couldn't be good. She hoped he would figure it out in time to tell her and Larry before their flight was over in about forty minutes. "Okay, team," Aims heard on the intercom, "here's the deal." Rick said, "SECNAV wants us to investigate the crash of a corporate jet at the executive airport that serves the Marco Island resort near Naples."

"What about NTSB, boss?" Larry, the team's utility guy, asked over the intercom. "Aren't they the ones to investigate civilian plane crashes?" Aims's question exactly.

"Yes," Rick said. "They usually are. But this one has special circumstances."

"Let me guess," Aims said. "Dead passengers who were high-ranking navy officers."

"Even Pentagon posted," Rick said.

Dead bodies in a plane crash troubled her. Once, she had almost been one herself. But she had always been fascinated by the process of finding the evidence and solving the mysteries of the case. Now her job consisted of finding out *why*—always the challenge. She liked that. Challenges felt better than structure.

Her silence was interrupted by Rick's voice in her headset.

"We'll probably know more when we get there, team," Rick said. "But three stars on the shoulder boards of one of the passengers was enough to get SECNAV's attention and send us to take the first look. NTSB may meet us there, but we're to be the first investigators. The report to SECNAV indicated that the crash might not be an accident. That's all we know at this point."

Rick reached out and touched Aims's arm. What was that frisson of … something? Their eyes met.

She nodded.

"Who made the report to SECNAV?" Larry asked over the intercom.

"Fire and rescue unit from the fire station right down the street. They got the first call. The lead member was a former navy master chief petty officer. He recognized the admiral's rank on the body in uniform."

"That's a pretty gutsy move," Larry responded. "Going straight to the top of the ladder."

"I'm sure there's more to the story," Rick said. "We'll probably find out what it is before this assignment is over.

"We're approaching the coordinates of the crash site, Aims. What about doing a flyover before we get to the airport itself?"

"Okay," Aims replied. "Larry, we're going low and slow. You want to activate the camera pod and see what we come up with?"

"On it, Skipper," Larry replied. Right now, he was the flight engineer and loadmaster. He would do photos and measurements while they were on the ground. He was a tall, skinny man with a shock of wayward, straw-colored hair. Aims and Rick had always been impressed with the workings of his mind. Orderly. Scary.

After receiving authorization from the regional air traffic control center, she made the changes required for flying lower and slower so the cameras mounted on the wing's pod could record the terrain below. Rick had binoculars to his face to get another set of eyes on what they might record.

The Osprey was still about a thousand yards from the airport perimeter when Rick said, "Tallyho. Ten o'clock, Larry."

"Got it," he replied. "Why don't we hover a little bit offset from it, Skipper?"

"On it now." Aims made the adjustments Larry requested. She

could see the blackened tail assembly several feet from what was apparently the main cabin of the plane. Looked like one of the engines had taken a hit. The wings had apparently flown off in opposite directions, enlarging the crash site. The main cabin and the cockpit had separated. Then Aims noticed flashes of light coming from a few yards away. Were those muzzle flashes?

"Rick," she called. "Four o'clock. Light flashes. Could we be in someone's sights?"

"Maybe. Take us to the airport and set us down. No need to join the crash site that way. We'll do the rest on the ground."

When the Osprey settled onto the tarmac, it looked like a circus. While Rick responded to another call on his cell phone, the team descended the rear ramp. A sheriff's deputy was still present, and the established crime scene perimeter began at the gate of the airport itself.

A black Lincoln town car limousine was sitting next to the chain-link fence, the driver's door open and a man in livery seated in it, one foot resting on the pavement. Lookie-loos crowded against the outside of the fence, and a local TV satellite truck and crew were arriving. The young deputy had his hands full maintaining the integrity of the crash site. The navy investigators were glad he was there. That was a job Aims was happy not to worry about.

As the team walked over to him to introduce themselves, Rick rejoined them. They would show a little bit of appreciation. It could help to defuse turf issues.

"Good morning, Deputy. I'm Special Agent Rick Holt, and these are my teammates, Lieutenant Commander Aims Wallace and Agent Larry Robb. We were sent from the navy office at Brunswick,

Georgia." All three displayed their badges and credentials to the deputy.

"Deputy Zach Taylor, Collier County Sheriff's Office. I was expecting the NTSB crew."

"While we were in the air," Rick said, "our boss told me that his boss, who is the secretary of the navy, was invited by the NTSB to assign our team to do the preliminary search here and to transport wreckage and other evidence back to our office in Georgia. We are to meet the Go team from Washington, DC, there. So we're it." Rick grinned at the deputy as he concluded their handshake.

"You mean no other feds are coming?"

"Not now anyway. So, what do we have?" Rick and the others clustered around the deputy, taking in the scene. "We see that you've established a perimeter for us. Great job. That really helps."

"Who's in the limo?" Aims asked.

"He's the chauffeur for the plane's owner. Name's White. He seems to be a sort of general gofer for Mr. Blackstone. White says that his boss got a call when they flew over Orlando with a position report and an ETA. Blackstone sent White over to meet the plane and his guests."

"Boss," Larry Robb interjected. "The NTSB sent the passenger list via SECNAV to my cell phone. Passengers were a three-star admiral by the name of James Carter and his aide, Captain Bryce Wilford. Pilot's name was Joe Grimes. Their flight plan was filed from an executive field near the Groton, Connecticut, navy base."

"Wait a minute," Taylor said. "Rescue said there was only one passenger—a high-ranking navy guy in addition to the pilot. They said both occupants of the wreckage had GSWs to the left temple. They said they didn't see any evidence of anyone else on board."

"Curiouser and curiouser," Aims murmured.

"Deputy," Rick said, "did you do any looking around the wreckage?"

"No, sir. It's quite a ways away, and a crowd was already beginning to gather. I felt that setting up and maintaining the perimeter was a higher priority."

"You were right," Rick said. "Good thinking." He turned to his team. "Aims, why don't you get a statement from our limo driver while Deputy Taylor guards the perimeter? Larry, let's get the Zodiac inflatable. You can take some more pictures. Bring the metal detector so we don't miss anything."

While the others went to the plane to prepare to inspect the wreckage, Aims walked toward the limo and driver.

"Mr. White," she said. "Hi. My name is Lieutenant Commander Amelia Wallace. I'm an investigator for the navy, and I'm part of the team assigned to find out what happened to your boss's plane. May I join you in the car?" Aims had her badge and identification ready to show him.

"Sure," he said. "But just call me White. Everyone does." The man showed some apparent hesitancy when he stepped out of the car, pulling the rear door open for Aims.

"Thank you, White," she said. After she stowed her ID in her jacket pocket, she sat on the rear seat. She slid over toward the center of the car and gestured for White to join her. "I know you talked to the sheriff's deputy, but I need to hear your statement firsthand. Do you mind if I record this?" She pulled a small recording device from her pocket. When he nodded, she turned on the recorder and placed it on the seat between them. She identified herself and White on the tape, with the date, time, and place of the recording.

"So, let's begin with your arrival here at the airport."

"Mr. Blackstone was expecting more guests for a week of fishing on the Gulf," White said. "He sent his plane to pick them up from an airport near the submarine base in Connecticut."

"Was that Admiral Carter?" Aims asked.

Yes, and his aide, Bryce Wilford," White replied. "Joe radioed that they had taken off at first light, so we were expecting them to arrive here around nine thirty this morning. Joe said he would let us know when he was over Orlando."

"Would the pilot be Joe Grimes?"

"Yes, ma'am. He's been flying for Mr. Blackstone about five years now."

"Mr. Blackstone must have trusted him."

"Yes, ma'am. Most of us have worked for Mr. Blackstone for a number of years. Mr. Blackstone makes us feel like a family, knowing each other well. We're going to really miss Joe." To Aims's eye, White's distress seemed real enough, but she knew that being the gofer for a powerful and wealthy man could give a person some acting skills.

"Okay," she said. "So, Joe called when he was over Orlando?"

"Yes, ma'am. Mr. Blackstone told me to give it about ten minutes and then come over here."

"What time did the call come in?" In addition to the recording, Aims was making notes on her phone.

"That was about nine twenty. I remember thinking how close that was to our estimate of the time they would get here."

"Good. When you got here, what was going on?"

"There was nobody around. I used Mr. Blackstone's key to unlock the gate to come in."

"Did you see anyone outside the fences? Any water activity? Like a small fishing boat or something?"

"No, no one. I always bring binoculars so I can look at the birds and other wildlife around here while I'm waiting. I've seen some awesome specimens."

"I can imagine." Aims smiled. "This seems to be a great area for that."

"Yes, ma'am. You know, the Ten Thousand Islands National Wildlife Refuge is just a few miles that way." He pointed toward the eastern boundary of the airport.

"No, I didn't know that," Aims replied. "But that doesn't surprise me. You're a sort of bird watcher then?"

"Yes, ma'am." He tapped a small notebook in his shirt pocket. "It's a great hobby. And it keeps me alert during long wait times."

"Good. What happened next? Were you the one who called the plane crash in to 911?"

"Yeah. I was looking off toward the Wildlife Refuge because I knew that Joe would be approaching from that direction. I had just caught sight of the Cessna when it looked like it flew into a fireball. Then parts of it were flying off in every direction. It was horrifying."

As Aims listened to White describe what he saw, she realized that she was getting the first indication of what had brought the small jet down. Could the fireball that White saw in front of the plane have been the fiery tail of a surface-to-air missile?

"Excuse me a moment, White," she said. "I need to speak to a member of my team for a second." She exited the limo on the passenger side and called Rick on her cell.

"What's up, Aims?"

"Rick, I just got something from the limo driver's observations. We could be looking for a heat-seeking surface-to-air missile."

"How so, Aims?"

"Listen to what he says." She held the recording device close to the cell phone and replayed the last couple of sentences of White's statement.

"Good catch, Aims. Larry and I will be on the lookout."

Aims returned to White in the limo. "Just a couple more questions. I know you've been here a while. I'm sorry for all of this, but there's a lot of red tape in a situation like this."

"It's okay," White replied. "I just talked to Mr. Blackstone, and he said I was to provide as much information as I could. He understands about all this."

"Great," Aims said. "Where is Mr. Blackstone now?"

"He and his wife and their other guests left yesterday for the offshore island he owns. It's his fishing retreat. It's only accessible by boat or air, and it's quite rustic, so they usually sleep aboard the yacht and camp out at the fishing lodge during the day."

"It must be quite a large yacht to accommodate the crew, family, and guests."

"Yes, ma'am. It is. Crew includes a chef, serving staff, and cabin attendants, as well as the captain and his staff. It involves most of the household staff. It even has a small boathouse and helipad so they can be provisioned during extended voyages."

"Wow. Awesome. I assume it must have satellite communications if you've just talked to him."

"Yes, ma'am. It does."

"Okay. Well, we're going to need a list of the staff who reside here on Marco Island and work at the house and on the yacht, as well as their contact information and length of service."

"That won't be a problem. I manage the household. I have that information at the house."

"Good," Aims said. "I'll call you and set up a time to meet you there as soon as we arrange ground transportation. It's looking like this investigation will be a little more complicated than we first thought."

She pocketed the business card White handed her and shook his hand. "We'll be in touch soon. Thank you so much. You've been helpful."

"You're welcome. My pleasure." White slid out of the limo and held out his hand to assist her departure. "Am I finished here?"

"Yes, you are. Thank you again. We'll see you later." Aims stepped back as White entered the limo and drove toward the airport gate. The deputy looked over at Aims, who nodded the okay for him to exit. Behind her, she heard the sound of the Zodiac's motor taking Rick and Larry around the wreckage.

❦

Out of the inflatable, Rick began to walk toward the wreckage. "First, Larry," he said, "tell me what we have."

"Okay. Who put up the yellow tape? Sheriff?"

"Nope. EMTs."

"Did they get all of the crash site?"

"We don't know yet. Not their job anyway. That's one of the things we're looking for right now. It's why we brought the metal detector. Talk to me about this crash site."

"Well, let me see. The pilot missed making the runway by a

pretty big margin. A thousand yards or more. Looks like the EMTs cut through the chain-link fence to get to the debris. Pretty large chunk of the tail assembly with the engines over here. Maybe the flight data recorders are still in it. Looks like a lot of fire damage, and one of the engines looks shredded. There could have been an explosion. We'll want to get that on the Osprey and back to our lab."

"Well," Rick said, "Aims just called to say the limo driver's report indicates a possible hit by a surface-to-air missile. Most likely heat-seeker. How would that fit with what we're seeing?"

"That would do it. That's scary. That changes this from a simple airplane accident to something else. Maybe even homegrown terrorism."

"That's another reason we're here. So," Rick said, "let's just walk around a bit before we check out the main cabin section over there."

"Do I still need to be on the lookout for wild life?"

"Maybe." Rick grinned. "We might have scared off most of them with all this activity."

"But you're not sure about that, are you? Could we have two-legged snakes in the grass?"

"We don't know, Larry. Remember the light flashes we saw on the way in. We need to be watching our six. If anyone was here, they could still be close by."

"Right, boss," Larry replied.

Just then, the ticking of the metal detector stopped their banter.

"Over here," Larry said. "They did miss something."

Rick slogged through the marsh toward him.

"What do you think it is, Larry?" Rick asked. He had already reached his own conclusion.

"Well, I'm no expert on military weapons," Larry replied, "but I think this is the launch tube from a surface-to-air missile. Whoever used it left in too big a hurry to pick it up. It was pretty well hidden in the high grass. EMTs missed it." He gestured toward the yellow tape perimeter that was strung a couple of yards away.

"Good catch, Larry. Snap it and bag it. Okay." Any hint of levity had gone from Rick's expression. "Now we have some solid proof of foul play. So, how did the culprits make their getaway?"

Larry looked around him thoughtfully. "If I were doing this, I'd use a Zodiac or small airboat. No place for tire tracks and plenty of small waterways to disappear into. The Gulf of Mexico is only a few minutes that way."

"I agree," Rick said. "I'm glad you're on the team with the good guys." Both of them were still gazing at the surrounding terrain when Larry suddenly lifted his camera off his chest and snapped a couple of quick shots. When Rick looked in the direction that Larry's camera was pointing, he caught another sudden flash of light. Looked like sunlight reflecting off something shiny. Could it be the lens of binoculars or a rifle scope? Silenced sniper shots? Larry had already snapped another couple of exposures.

"Did you catch 'em?" Rick asked quietly.

"Yeah, boss. Been seeing those for a few minutes now, haven't we? I think we do have some more wildlife in the weeds. Good idea to keep watching our six."

"Let's check out this section of the main cabin. The EMTs said they left the bodies of the crash victims in place. We'll take pictures," Rick said.

He started off after Larry, and his phone rang. Caller ID said it was Aims.

"Yeah, Aims. What's up?"

"I've just finished with White, the limo driver. He's going back to Blackstone's estate and will be compiling a list of employees and their work history. What did you find out about a possible SAM?"

Rick stepped in the lee of the cabin wreckage, away from the flashes of light he and Larry had noticed.

"We found the launch tube and some more evidence that some eyes could still be watching among the weeds."

"I've been thinking," Aims said.

"Well," Rick said, "that's always a good thing."

"I'm thinking," Aims went on, ignoring his comment, "we're going to need some time on the ground here, but this evidence needs to get back to base for analysis ASAP."

"I agree," Rick replied. "Were you thinking you would call Brunswick and fill them in? See if they want to send a ferry crew to take this evidence on the Osprey and leave us transport back?"

"Yeah. Then do you want me to join you out there?"

"No, Larry and I got this covered," Rick said. "When you get the ferry crew nailed down, you can make arrangements at the terminal office for tie-down space for the incoming craft. By then, Larry and I will be done, and we can have you bring the Osprey out here to winch the debris on board, ready to be taken back to Brunswick."

"Are you trying to protect me from viewing the remains of the victims?" There was a hint of bristle in her tone.

"Did you really want to view them?" Rick asked gently. "Larry and I can take pictures just as well as you can. Maybe even better."

"No," Aims replied. "I don't *want* to view them. But I do want to do my job, just like everyone else. You know that. Don't cut me any extra slack, Rick."

"Don't sweat it, Aims," Rick said. "You're carrying your weight.

Just make that call so we can load up the Osprey and get the evidence back to base. When Larry and I get back to you, we're going to need ground transport. You could call Enterprise too."

"Okay," Aims said. "You're the boss. I was already thinking about renting a car."

"And, Aims," Rick added, "watch your six. There could be eyes along the fence near you as well as out here in the weeds."

"Right," she said as she ended the call.

"Was this door open when the rescue crew got here?" Larry asked when Rick caught up to him. "Or did they open it?" He was standing next to the bottom of the stairs. "When we flew over it, it was open."

"According to our boss," Rick said, "the navy chief reported the door was open when they got here.

"Have you been inside yet?" Rick asked.

"No, boss. Thought I'd wait for you. Corroboration."

"Yeah, I know," Rick said. He raised his camera and took several shots of the slightly askew door stairs.

"Do we have to go in this way? Can we get in through the opening in the front?" Rick asked.

"I think we can," Larry replied. "I don't like the idea of disturbing possible evidence either."

"Looks like the missile hit the plane near one of the engines. That would confirm the possibility that it was a heat-seeker," Larry said. "Thickens the plot."

As he and Larry climbed into the wrecked main cabin, Rick wondered what he and the team were *really* dealing with. Who had brought this Cessna business jet down and why? Were they being watched? Could he protect Aims and Larry long enough to get answers? Could this mean a change in his relationship with Aims?

He and Aims had been best friends for seven years. Beyond that friendship, he figured she was out of his league. She was blue blood, and he was blue collar. But there had been a connection between them. He hoped that Aims was as aware of the attraction as he was. She had never given any indication of it, but neither had she ever displayed any indication of elitist thinking. Rick wondered why he'd been letting such a phony class distinction stop him from revealing his feelings to Aims all these years. Maybe it was time to roll the dice. Neither of them was getting any younger. If she rejected him, maybe he needed to cut his losses and move on.

That would have to be in the future. At this moment, all of their focus needed to be on this investigation. Something really bad appeared to be at work here. As he entered the wreckage, he sent up a prayer for wisdom and protection.

Chapter 2

Rick and Larry photographed the gunshot wounds on the admiral and the pilot as well as the evidence that something had once encircled the admiral's wrist but was no longer present in the aircraft wreckage. That was the only indication that there had been a third party aboard. The admiral's aide was listed on the passenger manifest. But where was he? What had happened to him? Between them, Rick and Larry agreed that leaving the bodies in place for transport back to the lab was preferable to moving them and placing them in body bags, especially since Aims had gotten the okay for a ferry crew, which was already en route.

The ferry crew would take the evidence back to base while the team kept up their investigation at the site. Rick and Larry finished the documentation at the wreckage, and Aims made the arrangements at the airfield's office for the tie-down of the small jet helicopter coming from Brunswick. She also called the Enterprise Rental agency in Naples to arrange for ground transport. A luxury SUV would allow them to be less obtrusive while offering them the versatility that could come in handy. By the time she finished that call, Rick and Larry were bringing the Zodiac into the Osprey.

"Finished?" she asked, ending her phone call.

"Yeah," said Larry. "Crank this truck up and let's get her loaded." Aims brought the Osprey back over the wreckage, and Rick and Larry winched the pieces of wreckage onto the hovering aircraft. It was a tight fit, but Larry was a skilled loadmaster, and they were able to button it down for the return trip to Brunswick field office. According to Aims's call to their boss, they still had several minutes to wait. So, only now could they consider what they were dealing with.

Larry drove the Enterprise driver back to his office in the SUV, and when he returned, they would pack it with the few personal items they had on the Osprey. The original plan had called for the team to be there only a few hours, so all of them were going to need to buy provisions.

Rick wandered off to the south perimeter fence of the airport parking lot and stared at the maze of waterways that led to the Gulf of Mexico a few miles away. He was still wondering if this assignment represented a turning point in his relationship with Aims—or with the navy, for that matter. He had a lot of options if he chose to look. He replayed the remark that Aims had made to him, "Don't cut me any extra slack."

It was a tough request to grant—more like impossible, even though Aims made that request often. If it came to that, caring about her would be a difficult habit to break. The image of her lying in the hospital bed like a broken doll, wires and tubes running out of her everywhere, with monitors beeping and squiggling marks on a screen haunted him. It was his first sight of her and had etched the image into his memory.

After being Brett Wallace's law clerk for several years, he understood Aims's pushing him away because of the similarity of his personality to her father's. He wondered if they'd ever get around that. But staying close to her felt right. It looked like an unsolvable dilemma. He didn't like that. It bothered him. A lot.

Aims watched Rick as he stared out over the watery landscape. One hand brushed absently over his close-cropped hair. Every time he did that, she wondered what went through his mind when he looked off into the distance like that. Whenever he was near, her attention was drawn to him. Though she insisted that they were just good friends, he always drew her in. She wanted to be near him. It always felt better. She replayed the moment Rick touched her hand on the flight here. What was the sensation she experienced? Rick had often touched her in passing. They were best friends, after all. There were no barriers between them. But the effect she had been experiencing recently was somewhat different. She couldn't define it and had tried to ignore it. Why? It wasn't a bad feeling. In fact, it seemed like a switch had been thrown. Added light, color, a sort of exhilaration. All of those were good. Why try to ignore those sensations?

Aims's musings were interrupted by the roar of a helicopter turbine engine approaching the airport. Aims, Rick, and Larry gathered by the Osprey as the small chopper settled onto the tarmac near them. The pilot shut down, and she and the two passengers got out. After exchanging salutes and signing for each other's aircraft, the ferry crew boarded the Osprey and took off. Aims boarded the small chopper and air taxied to their assigned spot. While she and

Larry tied down the helicopter, Rick checked them out with the airport manager, and they piled into the Escalade. Their first stop was to interview the former navy master chief who had notified SECNAV of the crash.

❧ ❧ ❧

Chief Cliff Orbison was a burly and grizzled veteran of navy deck gun mounts and local fire stations. His sun-darkened face looked like a road map of experience with the foibles of the officers and men he had met and dealt with through his lifetime. His once red hair was still there but thinning now and mottled with white.

When Larry pulled the Escalade onto the apron in front of the small fire and rescue substation, the doors were still open, and Orbison and a coworker were rolling hoses after washing down the two units that had responded to an earlier callout. Orbison walked over to meet the investigators as they got out of the rental vehicle.

"Howdy, folks. Can we help y'all?" His bearing and demeanor seemed to demand that he be addressed by his former navy rank.

Rick held out his hand. "Special Agent Rick Holt, Chief. NCIS. This is Lieutenant Commander Amelia Wallace and Agent Larry Robb. SECNAV sent us to look over the wreck you reported. Got a minute?"

"Sure. Cliff Orbison," he said as he shook hands with Rick and Larry and saluted Aims.

"Old habits die hard, don't they, Chief?" Aims smiled as she returned the salute.

"Yes, ma'am, they do," Orbison replied. "Thirty years in the navy can do that to ya. But respect for women folk came from my daddy's knee back in the hills of Kentucky."

"Did the navy wash out your accent, Chief?" Aims asked.

"Mostly, ma'am. That 'n' fifteen years here in south Florida.

"This way." He turned and led them into the station to a small room containing a scarred, battered table and rickety chairs. A large coffee urn sat on the counter nearby with an assortment of mismatched and stained mugs. Orbison picked up a mug and gestured to the three investigators.

"Navy brew?" Rick questioned. When Orbison nodded, Rick said, "Sure thing, Chief. Been a few years since my Marine Corps days, but I learned to respect swabbie coffee." Orbison grinned as he poured three mugs and filled one for himself.

As they seated themselves, Aims placed her recorder on the table.

"Protocol, Chief. Okay?"

After Orbison's nod and Aims's identification of the recording, Rick tapped on the screen of his cell phone and then looked at Orbison.

"Do you mind repeating what you told the NTSB and SECNAV, Chief? I want to make sure they got everything right."

For the next several moments, Orbison repeated essentially the same information that had been relayed to the team from the NTSB report and from SECNAV through their boss at Brunswick. It wasn't much.

"Do I understand that the stair door into the main cabin wreckage was open when you got there, Chief?" Rick asked.

"Yes, sir."

"Did you enter the wreckage that way?" he asked.

"No, sir. Didn't wanna compromise any evidence. Crawled in from the front o' the wreckage."

"Was White, Mr. Blackstone's driver, at the airport while you were there?" Aims asked.

"Yeah," Orbison replied. "He was there when we got there. Dispatch said he was the guy that called 911."

"Did you interview him?" Rick asked.

"Yeah, I did." Aims and Rick waited for a few beats and then looked at each other when Orbison did not add any other comment.

"What's your take on him and Blackstone?" Aims asked finally.

After another long pause, Orbison cleared his throat. "I don' wanta color *yer* take before ya talk to 'em," he said.

Larry watched the interchanges between the three military types.

Perhaps he figured if he waited long enough, what he was missing would become clear. Maybe he just hoped so.

"Well," said Rick, "that's probably what we should do next." He turned to Aims. "Didn't you say that Blackstone had authorized White to provide us with information on the household staff?"

Aims nodded.

The four stood, and Orbison collected the used coffee mugs and placed them in the sink. Then he led them back to the front of the substation. "Where're y'all stayin'?" he asked as they approached the large open door in front of the fire trucks.

They had just stepped out into the sunlight when something pinged off the rear of the Escalade. The hiss of escaping air accompanied the settling of the left rear wheel. Instinctively, Rick grabbed Aims's hand and pulled her down. Orbison did the same to Larry. But Rick, Orbison, and Aims were already scanning the surrounding terrain, looking for the threat. Although thoroughly frightened, Aims's training demanded that she participate in the threat assessment. What was going on here? Were they already getting pushback from whoever brought down Blackstone's plane? Evidently, the admonition to "watch our six" was more than just a military catch phrase. How many were there? Where were they?

"Silenced?" asked Aims.

"Yeah," said Rick and Orbison in unison.

"Sniper," Aims guessed. "From where?"

"From the angle," Rick said, "I'd guess probably from one of those buildings across the street. In spite of its harmless-appearing landscaping, the various roof heights in that mall would make for an ideal sniper nest." Rick slowly got to his feet. "Whoever he is, he's good. That's a long shot, but I think he's gone."

"Wasn't meant ta kill," Orbison said. "If he'd wanted ta kill, one of us'd be dead. Hit what he aimed at. Probably just wanted ta slow ya down."

"I'd guess he did that," Larry groused. "These rentals don't come with spares." He pulled out his cell phone.

"Wait," Orbison said. "There's a tire shop right next door. We gotta deal with 'em ta come over and fix our flats when we need it. I'll ask them ta help ya out here."

"Thanks, Chief. Appreciate it."

"Listen," said Orbison. "Y'all didn't say where y'all're staying while y'all're in town. Looks to me like y'all're gonna need a secure place ta recharge your batteries. Check yer sixes. Y'all got such a place?"

"No," said Aims. "We hadn't gotten that far yet. This is breaking so fast we're still reacting. You have some place in mind?"

"How about stayin' on a boat for a few days? I gotta boat docked at a marina near here. I'm part owner of the marina with my daughter. We own the boat docked close to my slip, 'n' my girl and I could help watch fer ya. I work twenty-four hours on and forty-eight hours off. My shift is up in a couple of hours. That'd give ya time ta interview White at Blackstone's estate, and then y'all could come back here 'n' follow me home. Think about it and lemme know. For now, y'all need ta get that left rear tire fixed 'n' an appointment set up with White. I'll be here when y'all're ready."

"This jarhead thinks that suggestion from a swabbie makes sense." Rick grinned. Aims and Larry stood with amused smiles.

"Okay," Larry said. "Let's get this buggy back on the road again while Aims makes a date with the limo driver."

Aims already had her cell phone up and waiting for White to answer.

❦ ❦ ❦

The slug recovered from their flat tire was in the console between the front seats. It would go to the lab. It might be a link to the killer of the navy personnel, so it was a valuable piece of evidence.

"Stop here, Larry," Rick said. "We'll get out and look around the neighborhood while Aims talks to White. It could give us a feel for this neighborhood."

"Right, boss," Larry replied. "You never know what will give you a clue about someone until you look around the area where he lives." He drew the Escalade to a stop and got out. Aims went around and slid behind the wheel. She shifted into drive and eased into the entrance to the estate.

White answered the door, and Aims noticed a subtle difference in his demeanor. *Okay. What's the difference?* She started with his appearance. For one thing, he had changed out of his chauffeur's livery and now wore a button-down dress shirt, open at the collar. His dark slacks were sharply creased. *I've seen this before. Momma called it feeling home turf advantage. And some arrogance. Not at all the same person I met at the airport, where White seemed to be a self-effacing bird watcher. Now his manner is more self-assured and controlling.*

Aims's gaze swept the elegant entrance with its high coffered ceilings as White led her into the sitting area beyond. Through the archway, she could see a tiled solarium containing a mosaic fountain, water spraying. The solarium wrapped the back of the house next to the waterway. The long dock was empty at the moment, but White had said the Blackstone family was fishing aboard the yacht in the Gulf. Off to one side, she had a glimpse of tennis courts and a helipad where a small chopper was tied down.

Nice place. But my elitist momma would consider it gaudy. She'd say it looked like it was supposed to reflect affluence, but instead, it's just a tasteless display of wealth. What was her saying? Oh, yes, "Class is not purchased, married, or inherited. It is an acquired taste." Whoever decorated this house doesn't have it yet. Such snobbery and putting on airs. This is why I decided on a career as a US Navy pilot instead of a life of cotillions, debutante balls, and annual home tours.

That's what had changed in White, she decided. *He's an actor on a fancy set.* As she had before, she placed her recorder on the coffee table in front of her, after identifying herself and White again.

"May I offer you a refreshment, Commander?" White asked as he handed her a few sheets of paper.

"No, thank you, White," Aims responded as she glanced at the paper to see what sort of information was being provided. "I want to take this with me. Okay? The team and I will need to do some background checks to look for clues to why Mr. Blackstone's plane was brought down."

"Are you saying that the crash was not an accident?" White's face darkened.

This question set off alarm bells that Aims chose not to ignore. It was not just an interested question. *Closer to the vest, Aims.*

"Of course, I cannot comment on an ongoing investigation," Aims replied. "But we can't rule anything out at this point. I did mention that this was shaping up to be a little more complex than what was first imagined."

"You mentioned your team. How many investigators are working in the area?" White's agitation was slowly increasing. "Where are they now?"

"Well, so far, just the three of us you saw come off the plane at the airport," Aims said. "At the moment, the other two are strolling the neighborhood, just to get a feel for Mr. Blackstone's surroundings. Sometimes that kind of exploration is helpful to our investigation. Please don't be concerned. We've operated in all sorts of neighborhoods. We will not be an embarrassment to Mr. Blackstone by our presence or our behavior. But in investigations of this sort, you never know where you'll find a significant clue."

"How will they know when you're finished here?" White was still frowning.

"We're in constant touch by cell phone," she assured him.

"So, just three people are on your team?"

"Well," said Aims, "as I said, right now, no more than us three. Each of us is cross-trained to provide a broad spectrum of skills in order to back each other up. We try to keep the number small. It helps keep expenses down. I'm sure you make those same kinds of decisions in your role of household manager. Budget control is sure to be a large part of any manager's daily concern." Aims's smile was open and noncommittal.

White's response was an ambiguous sound in his throat.

"So," said Aims. "We still need to talk to Mr. Blackstone. I will call you when we need to make arrangements for that visit. How long did you say he and his guests will be out on the Gulf?"

"They will be there the rest of the week. But with Joe gone, we will not be able to provide transport to get you out there."

"That won't be a problem, White," Aims said. "You said the yacht has a helipad. We have a small chopper at the executive airport that we can use. When we're ready for that interview, I'll contact you for the coordinates of the yacht or island. Will you need to clear our visit ahead of time?" She slipped her hand into her jacket pocket and hit the speed dial on her phone so Rick would know she'd be coming out of the house.

"It would be a good idea. That way, Mr. Blackstone can be sure to be on the yacht when you plan to arrive. Call me first, and I'll arrange the details." White rose to his feet in a clear signal that the interview was at an end. Aims followed his lead. When he opened the front door to usher her out, both Rick and Larry were standing by the Escalade waiting for her. If the sniper shot had been White's doing, he wasn't displaying overt hostility now. Aims turned and shook White's hand before moving to the passenger door, which Rick held open for her. Larry slid into the driver's seat as Rick sat in the rear seat. Rick gave a little salute to White as they drove out of the hedged-in courtyard onto the street.

As they headed back to the fire station, Aims tried to decide how she felt about the interview with White. There was no mistaking the edge of … something that had developed in his responses to her. Was it possible that he was involved in the destruction of the Cessna? Had he even masterminded the scenario? Did he pose a threat to her, Rick, and Larry? A little shiver ran up her spine as she turned her attention to the information he had given her. When they were settled into a base, she would play the recordings of her interviews with White for Rick and Larry. She could rely on Rick's judgment as backup for her own impressions. In fact, it occurred to her that she relied on Rick for a lot of things. *Do I rely on him too much? It feels like I really need him.* Was she praying now? Hadn't she decided that God probably wasn't too interested in what she had to say? Had she changed her mind? Over the years of her association with Rick, she had scoffed at his references to prayer and divine intervention. But maybe, without realizing it, she had come to trust his faith, even emulate his practice of praying occasionally. To wish for a return to her previous faith. To be able to reach out and find the Holy Spirit's presence when she felt inadequate. How had that happened? Did God really care about her? Did He really have a plan for her? Maybe He *was* listening to her. As fantastic as it seemed, maybe there *was* some ultimate benefit to be had from all of this.

Chapter 3

Larry pulled the Escalade onto the apron next to the fire station. Aims and her team got out as Orbison came to greet them.

"Hi, Chief," Rick said. "Is that offer of a boat at your marina still open?"

"Sure. I'll call my daughter, Maisie, and have her get the paperwork ready." He turned toward the locker area inside the station, reaching for his cell phone. He stopped suddenly and turned back toward the three investigators.

"Y'all had lunch yet?"

"Not yet," Aims replied for the team. "Other than some coffee on the Osprey and the coffee with you, we've been too preoccupied to add anything else to it since we got here."

"Okay," Orbison replied. "I'll have Maisie take out some steaks from my freezer, and we'll grill after we get y'all settled in. Okay?"

"Hope they're big." Larry grinned. "I'm pretty hungry."

"A chronic problem," Rick observed, and they all chuckled. Orbison made his phone call and signed out.

Larry aimed the nose of the Escalade at the tow package on

the rear bumper of Orbison's older pickup as they headed down the road. It was a deceptively straight road that seemed to lead nowhere. Narrow strips of sea grapes bordered the roadway, and Aims could see canals through the foliage on either side. There were frequent glimpses of small motor boats containing one or two fishermen cast fishing in the waterways. It was evident that independent fishing was a serious business in this part of southwest Florida, right up there in importance with yachting. Aims wondered what else occupied a prominent place in the area's tourist industry. Certainly golfing, if the presence of a world-class golf course on Marco Island was any indication. She had wondered about that when they passed it on the way to Blackstone's estate.

The street sign said they were headed for the Isle of Capri when Orbison led them into a right turn. After a short distance, the road broke into the open. It was bordered by a large, landscaped parking lot fronting what looked like a high-end, exclusive shopping mall.

Aims noted a large regional grocery market, a couple of service stations, an auto-repair business, and a large market proclaiming to be The Ship's Store. The marina itself provided parking spaces and storage facilities for a wide variety of cruisers and sailboats of all sizes, along with a fully equipped and active dry dock with a boat lift that allowed owners to transport their crafts directly from storage space to the water. The parking lot also contained a scattering of recreational vehicles, so the boat owners probably did some land cruising as well.

Adjacent to the spacious and attractive office was a small, modern Laundromat and a large outdoor commons area complete with potted shrubs, flowering trees, party lights, and lanterns for evening picnics and parties.

Beyond the attractive adult playground was a large, glittering blue pool bordered by a well-equipped children's playground with a sandbox, traditional swings and slides, and climbing structures of all shapes and sizes. A private beach had been created nearby and boasted lounges, umbrellas, and portable windbreaks.

After they parked, the team joined Orbison on the way to the office.

"Wow," Aims said to Orbison. "This is quite a resort you have here."

"Thanks," Orbison replied. "Most of it is Maisie's doin'. She said she was stoppin' short of a full-service hotel and a high-end restaurant. Anyone wants that can travel down the road a piece to the Marriott or Hilton. They're surrounded by seafood and steak houses in all price ranges."

"Sounds like a smart woman," Aims said. "Must take after her dad."

"Thanks. She's smart."

Then Orbison grumped. "Her choice in men leaves a lot ta be desired."

"Well, then," Rick observed quietly as they approached the office door, "I guess it's a good thing she didn't have a choice when it came to dads."

"I guess you're right," Orbison said and pulled the door open.

The marina office was a pleasant surprise. Aims did not have a wide experience with marinas, but the ones she had visited were usually a cramped hodgepodge of activities occupying as little space as possible. This marina office was spacious and well lit, with windows on all sides as well as pot lights in the ceiling. The ambience suggested to Aims that the people at this marina had time to listen to customers, find out what they needed, and help them get it. Friendly. That was it. It felt friendly.

The woman behind the counter could only be Orbison's daughter, Maisie. She had the same mass of curly hair, but hers still retained all of its youthful fire, and so did her demeanor as she dealt with her disgruntled customer. She disarmed him with her courtesy and willingness to resolve his problem. His wife had watched the exchange with a somewhat bemused smile, and both walked away, obviously satisfied.

When Orbison and the team entered, Maisie lifted an acknowledging finger without interrupting her conversation with her customers. As they left the counter, and the office was momentarily without any others, she turned her attention to her father and those accompanying him.

"Hi, Dad. Are these our new tenants for the *Lindy Lou?*"

"Hi, Mizz Maisie," Orbison replied. "These're our new tenants." He motioned the team forward and made introductions.

As she shook hands in greeting, she glanced at her dad. "From the looks of her uniform, I'd say one of them outranks you, Chief." Her cobalt eyes sparkled in laughter. "How is that going to go?"

"Probably won't matter." Aims chuckled. "But we'll cross that bridge if and when we come to it.

"This is quite a place you have here. I'm really impressed."

"Thanks, Commander. Dad and I have put a lot of work into it. And it's all been a labor of love. Dad had me out on the water early in my life, and I love it as much as he does. I like to share that with others."

"It shows," Rick commented. "Your dad doesn't know it, but I spent eight years in the Marine Corps after I grew up around the waterfront in Baton Rouge. This feels like home."

"Wow, Dad," Maisie said, nudging her dad with an elbow. "You really hit the jackpot. A lady superior officer and an ex-jarhead. How'd you do that?"

"Knock it off, Mizz Maisie. These're armed federal agents. Ya don't want either one of us on their bad side."

"Yeah? What's up?"

"Have the scanner on this mornin'?"

"Yes. Oh, is this related to the business jet crash you were called out to?"

"This is the team that's lookin' into it."

"I didn't know NTSB had ex and serving military members."

"We're from a sister agency," Rick said. "We're filling in as a favor between our agencies' directors."

Maisie spent a long moment scrutinizing the three newcomers and her dad.

"Okay. I think I catch the drift. No problem.

"I did what you asked in your call, Dad," she said, turning to Orbison. "Including defrosting some steaks. This guy"—she motioned to Larry, who had remained silent through all of the conversation—"looks like he could eat his weight in rib eyes and not gain an ounce."

Larry grinned. "Well, ma'am," he said, "I haven't tried that yet, but it sounds like a fun thing to do."

"Down, boy," Orbison demurred. "Not today. Today, ya get the same rations as everybody else." The general laughter erased any lingering tension that had hung over them like a cloud since the sniper shot at the fire station. Orbison shoved the paperwork over in front of Rick, who signed for their stay aboard the *Lindy Lou* and then shoved it back to Maisie. Orbison then picked up the keys, motioned with his head, and led them outside past the customers' play areas to an area of boat slips somewhat separated from the main marina. There they saw a few slips where some boats and yachts of varying sizes were secured.

Tied up on their left, Rick recognized the shape of a converted Coast Guard motor lifeboat with a virtual antennae farm perched on the top of the main cabin. It was painted a gleaming white with the water line marked by a rich turquoise. Along the bow was her name, *Maisie Mae,* in sedate gold script.

"Wow," Rick said. "Now *that's* my dream boat. Former Coast Guard motor lifeboat. Right?"

Orbison's eyes twinkled. "Yer time along the waterfront in Baton Rouge was well spent, jarhead. That she is. And she's mine. So stop droolin'." He gestured to the boat moored across the waterway, her transom pointing toward the *Maisie Mae's* transom. The team followed Orbison's lead along the walkway toward the boat he indicated.

Although the super structure was also painted a gleaming white, her water line was marked in burgundy, and she was a few feet shorter that the *Maisie Mae.* She, too, had a crown of antennae atop what had been the wheelhouse, and her transom read *Lindy Lou, Naples, Florida, USA.*

"Y'all'll have to make do with her sister craft. Can you handle it?" Orbison asked.

"I think so." Rick grinned. "She would be my second choice anyway. She's also a former Coast Guard lifeboat, right? How did you get these pretty ladies anyway?"

"A long story," Orbison replied. "One better told while watching the sun set into the Gulf." He stepped onto the deck of the *Lindy Lou.* "Fer now, we get under cover. We been out in the open too long."

At that reference to the sniper's shot to their rear tire, the good feeling engendered by the banter between Orbison and Rick faded like a shade drawn. Aims shivered with the sudden chill that had nothing to do with the ambient temperature. When she glanced at Larry, she saw an answering frown as his gaze flickered away from her and outside toward the sunlit vista of water, boats, and children at play.

Aims was the one who spoke first.

"Right, Chief. Thanks. We'll get settled in and check in with the home office. Then we'll join you on the *Maisie Mae* to get those steaks going. If we don't get some food into Larry pretty soon, it could get ugly." She attempted a smile she did not feel as she returned the former navy chief's salute and headed below. Rick and Larry shook Orbison's hand and followed her.

Better than the other members on his team, Rick Holt had the background and experience to appreciate what Cliff Orbison had done with the lifeboat. He saw where Orbison had turned the utilitarian rescue boat into a comfortable but compact living space, demonstrating a knowledge of marine engineering as well as the eye and heart of an artist.

The team explored their new quarters. The captain's quarters near the prow were assigned to Aims, while Rick and Larry claimed the guest room. Beyond Aims's quarters was a dogged down hatch providing a watertight seal. They opened it and saw a small compartment with gauges mounted on the forward bulkhead, encircled by monitor screens. A bench along one side provided seating for its occupants. As the door opened, a red light came on, reminding Aims of the red, battle-lit combat information center aboard the aircraft carrier where she had served.

Back in their rooms, they dropped their backpacks and returned to the salon, where Larry plugged them into the sophisticated electronics aboard the *Lindy Lou* and made contact with their office in Brunswick.

Aims emailed the list of employees from Blackstone's estate so that the computer geeks could do the background checks, along with the ones on Blackstone's yacht as well as the passengers listed on the plane that had crashed. Then she and the others listened to her recordings of her times with White.

After that, Rick, Larry, and Aims clustered around the webcam as they Skyped the secure communications center. As expected, when the connections were made, they had a split screen display with Brunswick and SECNAV's office in the Pentagon in Washington. Aims was jarred when she realized that less than two hours had elapsed from the time the Osprey left the Marco Island airport and now. She realized that Laura Kent, their lab technician, had probably barely begun her investigation of the wreckage, and the medical examiner would probably still be in the early stages of his postmortem examination of the two bodies.

Rick reported what they had experienced, and their superior officers listened without comment. The report of the sniper attack only garnered a wordless hum. When he told them of Orbison's offer of a safe haven and promise to watch their sixes, Admiral Johnson, secretary of the navy, nodded approvingly. Rick had Aims report about her conversations with White and how Blackstone was out at sea on his yacht with an unspecified number of guests. She mentioned the preliminary idea of using the small helicopter at the airport to get there and back.

"Okay, team," the admiral said. "What do you know about Carter's aide, Wilford? Has he or his body turned up yet?"

"No, sir," Rick replied. "But we haven't had a chance to do an in-depth search of the crash area yet. Larry and I didn't spend a lot of time there, because we were getting indications that we could be under surveillance. I had hoped that we would have a chance to go back for a more thorough search, but this surveillance thing needs to be addressed first."

"I have a thought, Severin," the admiral said, addressing the director of the Brunswick office. "Why don't we hire former Master Chief Cliff Orbison as a civilian contractor for security and assistance with logistics? We could have him request a few days' leave from his job with the Naples Fire Department—as long as it takes. He will have charts on the boat where he lives, and he can provide transport anywhere within the Ten Thousand Islands area. I don't want to interfere with your crew's operation in any way, but I've known Orbison for a long time, and he seems to have already taken an interest in providing security for them. Talk it over and let me know."

"I will, sir," Collier replied.

"Okay. I'll let you get on with it. Keep me in the loop." The admiral's image faded, and the screen refocused to show the single connection between them and their boss.

Severin Collier, the Brunswick office operations manager, thought for a minute before tossing the ball to Rick.

"How does SECNAV's idea grab you, Holt?"

"It could work, sir. We're invited to grilled steaks when we get done here. He's right across the waterway. We can ask him. We'll call you back in an hour or so and let you know what we work out. How is that?"

"Good, Holt. Do you have anything else?"

"I'm sure that Laura and her cohorts haven't had time to gather much information from the wreckage and bodies. We're particularly interested in what she can tell us about the missile launch tube. We did recover the sniper bullet from our tire. We'll find a way to get it to you ASAP. As soon as we feed Larry and can discuss this contractor proposition with Orbison, we're going to see what we can turn up, if anything, about Wilford."

"If Orbison is amenable to being a water taxi driver, I assume you would rather we made the visit to Blackstone's yacht by water and not by air. Actually, I sort of like that idea better myself."

"What's your take on this guy, Orbison?" Collier asked.

With a slight grin, Rick replied, "He's seems pretty squared away for a squid. We've already placed our safety in his hands, and I think it was a good decision."

"Good. You all watch your sixes. I don't like where this seems to be headed."

When all parties were in agreement, Larry shut down their communications link. "Can we go get something to eat now?" His eyebrows were raised in question.

✢～✤～✣

Aims worked at the small food prep station, preparing a salad to go with the grilled steaks, baked potatoes, and corn on the cob. She glanced around the efficient but beautiful galley and had to marvel again at the artistry of the remodel of the former Coast Guard vessel, turning it into an elegant and functional home. Orbison, Rick, and Larry stood around the gas grill, while Orbison gave them the details on the changes he had made to the former motor lifeboat. At one point, he took the whole team topside to give them a look at the electronics that the *Maisie Mae* boasted. Not only did he have the capability to talk to military communications satellites, but he also had an array of underwater scrutiny to prevent the approach of attack from below the water line. The ever-vigilant Orbison had also added a depth charge launcher, which could be stowed when not needed.

Rick and Aims glanced at each other in silent communication, but neither broached the subject of Orbison's taking a subcontractor's role in their investigation until all of them, including Larry, had had their fill of the delicious meal.

As the four of them sat back, empty plates cleared and iced tea glasses refreshed, Rick tossed out the first pitch.

"You know, Chief," he began, "we checked in with our bosses before we came over from the *Lindy Lou*. Our boss in Brunswick also had Admiral Johnson from the Pentagon in the loop with us."

"How's my buddy, the admiral, doin'?" Orbison said. "Did ya know we've known each other since way back when? He was just a green ensign then."

"That rumor has been afloat," said Aims, a smile playing at the corners of her mouth. Orbison responded to her with a grin.

"The admiral seemed to appreciate that you have offered us a safe haven," Rick continued.

"Yeah," Larry said. "We told him you had steaks on the menu. We'll have to let him know that you know your way around a grill.

It was great, Chief. Let me know when you feel the urge to grill again." He patted his tummy.

"Okay, Stringbean, I might do that."

"Anyway," Rick said, regaining focus of the conversation, "in the exchange of information, it was noted that some searching of the Ten Thousand Islands area needs to be done, as well as the visit to Blackstone's yacht. Admiral Johnson raised the option of having a civilian boater, with knowledge and charts of the area, be our water taxi driver and security advisor. He thought you might be amenable to taking a leave from the fire station to sign on for that role. What say you, Chief?"

Orbison tapped a forefinger against his chin while contemplating each member of the team in turn. Finally, he drew in a deep breath and said, "I think I wanna agree to this crazy proposition.

"But if I'm goin' ta provide y'all's security, there have to be some rules. Fer instance, if we're away from the marina, then I will be watchin' y'all's backs with a lot of different systems. Lemme ask ya, did y'all explore the *Lindy Lou?*"

They nodded.

"Notice the waterproof hatch forward of the cabin I assume you assigned to the commander?"

Again, they nodded.

"While we're moored here in the marina, we can't be sure that there'll be no attempts on y'all's lives. I mean, the sniper fired on you in broad daylight, across a busy street, and while you were parked in front of our fire station. Whoever is after ya isn't afraid to take some big risks. A marina filled with civilians and their boats and shoppers won't slow 'em down. If they come here, I wouldn't recommend tryin' to find shelter off the boats. So, we're gonna need a plan, executed at a one-word signal, an' no hesitation on anyone's part. When that signal's made and y'all're on the *Lindy Lou*, y'all'll head immediately to that safe room forward of the commander's cabin. Signal's gonna be 'Vault.' It's been reinforced against damage by mines or torpedoes and as secure as I could make it. Agreed?"

"I see now why SECNAV thought you'd be a good security strategist," Rick said.

"Thanks," Orbison replied. "Goes with the job of providin' safe havens for people who need 'em. The *Maisie Mae*'s got a room jus' like the *Lindy Lou's* in her prow.

"Now, Commander, I want to hear your take on White. I know that you probably didn't see Blackstone, but I wanna know what yer impression of White is."

Aims had been anticipating this question from Orbison ever since they departed from the Blackstone estate on Marco Island. She had some experience with some very astute chief petty officers, and most of them did not suffer fools gladly. She sat for a moment, trying to formulate a coherent pattern from the thoughts and impressions that swirled in her mind when she thought about White.

"Knowing that you were going to ask me that doesn't make this any easier, Chief," she finally replied. "I have had some training in behavioral psychology and reading body language, but I never saw White interact with anyone except me, so I'm not sure how accurate my impressions are."

"Aims," Rick said, "you're a good interrogator. Don't sell yourself short. Your assessments are good. That's why I asked you to interview White in the first place."

"Okay, Commander," Orbison said. "Lemme hear what ya think."

"Well," Aims said, "I think White is something of a chameleon."

"Why d'ya say that?"

"The man I interviewed at the airport seemed to be self-effacing and ingenuous. The man who answered the door at Blackstone's estate was much more assertive and sort of territorial."

"Okay. I buy that. What else?"

"It occurred to me at the time that working for a wealthy, powerful employer for any length of time could turn a person into a pretty accomplished actor. My very proper southern mama would characterize his behavior as putting on airs and using the opulence of his surroundings to impress."

"But he did provide the information you requested concerning Blackstone's employees," Rick said.

"Yes, he did. He had the list of employees ready for me, but remember, he was a little disturbed to find out that you and Larry were exploring the neighborhood. You heard him try to find out what we would be doing as part of our investigation. That raised some red flags for me."

"How so, Commander?" Orbison asked.

"I thought he was trying to maintain a level of control over Blackstone and the household in general. More than would be expected for someone with the title of estate manager.

"I think I slipped up when I mentioned that we thought something or someone had brought down Mr. Blackstone's plane, but when he pounced on that, I tried to respond noncommittally. I think he knows we are suspicious, but I think he doesn't know exactly what our suspicions are. I should have played it closer to my vest. We'll just have to wait and see what, if anything, he'll do about that."

Orbison eyed Aims for a long moment. He glanced at Rick and said, "I gotta hand it to ya, Holt. She nailed him right between the eyes. Best description of that weasel I've ever heard. And summed up with such elegant language. Must be what ya get when ya send navy officers ta college." His grin took all of the sting out of his comment.

Aims's color rose somewhat, and both Larry and Rick nodded in agreement.

"She's good, Chief," Rick responded. "That's why she's my ex-oh."

"You are very close to the line, there, marine," Aims said, without heat or rancor. "Don't get too carried away with the title of team leader."

"Yeah," Larry piped up. "We're all working stiffs here."

Now Orbison's grin was broad. "Ya walked right inta that, marine," he said.

"I guess I did," Rick said. "Sometimes it goes that way."

"So, what about it, Chief? Do we have a water taxi driver and security officer for the duration of our investigation here?"

"Yeah," Orbison agreed with a drawl. "While I could do without the surface-to-air missiles and .22-caliber gunshot wounds to the temple, I could enjoy the change of pace of workin' with you crazy guys. Count me in.

"Tell me, what kinda equipment will we need? Any y'all dive? Scuba or snorkel? The *Maisie Mae* can handle that. Some of my buddies in the Coast Guard made sure I had charts of the entire Ten Thousand Islands area. We've already marked some of the privately owned islands. I think Blackstone's is one of 'em."

"Yeah," Rick said. "Larry and I have worked some underwater salvage projects in the past. Aims has too." Turning to her, he said,

"Would you mind getting Collier to work on the chief's independent contractor paperwork?"

Orbison said, "Before you've done that, Commander, I'll give y'all a detailed tour of the *Mae*'s amenities. You'll want ta transfer over to 'er this evenin' sometime. We'll set up watch schedules an' stuff."

While Aims began to clear up the galley, she had a thought. *There'll be several hours of determined planning, shopping, and logistics before we can settle in for the night. Even then, I imagine peaceful sleep is probably not much more than a faint hope.*

Chapter 4

And she was right. After the process of enrolling Orbison as a civilian contractor into the paperwork mill at Brunswick and the fast tour of the *Mae*'s interior and technical capabilities, the team headed for the shopping area surrounding the marina to augment the sparse provisions they had brought with them.

"We'll be a yachtin' party tourin' the islands providin' bird and wildlife sanctuary. We'll leave the marina early dawn," Orbison said. "This'll shorten the hours of night watch. If it gives an unpleasant surprise ta whoever might come lookin' for us to find us gone, so much the better."

It seemed to Aims that she had barely put her head on the pillow in her small cabin when she heard Rick's knock on the door.

"Reveille, Aims."

"Okay, Rick. I'm coming."

It was that darkest hour before sunrise when Aims made her way onto the bridge. They had cleared the boat slips in the marina and were passing the channel markers leading into the Gulf of Mexico. Orbison had topped off the fuel tanks the night before, and the special solar panels were wide awake and awaiting the sun. Radar antennae and sonar receivers were active, and Rick had already made the communications check with Brunswick via the encrypted military satellite that handled secure communications for all the US military installations located on or near the Florida peninsula. Larry handed her a cup of coffee.

"Thanks, Larry," she said as she joined Rick at the chart table. "What's the plan?"

"Chief and I thought we'd start off by skirting Marco Island, passing under the bridge for State Route 92, and then exploring the waterways southeast of the airport. Our draft is shallow, only four and a half feet, and where the charts show shallower depth, we'll use the Zodiac. What we're looking for right now is the missile launch site and any evidence of the whereabouts of Bryce Wilford. If he bailed before the plane hit the ground and is still alive, where is he? Someone had to have picked him up and given him a ride out of the marsh. If he's dead, where is his body? And what caused his death? I think those are the first questions we need to find the answers to."

"Those and who's responsible for all this," Aims said.

"Right," Rick said. "That too."

Aims took her cup of coffee and descended to the main deck, edging past the main cabin and onto the prow. It would take them several hours to get to the search area. She was glad she had gotten a long-sleeved, hooded T-shirt and long pants to cover her swimsuit. When the sun was up and the air warmed up, she would shed them, enhancing the picture of carefree boaters to whoever might be looking. She lifted her face into the cool predawn breeze marking the boat's speed. Her heart lifted too at the beauty of her surroundings. As long as one had to work for a living, this was the way to do it. *On a day like this, I'm glad not to be chained to a desk in a law office. Thank you, Lord, for this. Please be with us and protect us from whatever or whoever is out here. Help us find out what is going on here.* Okay. There it was again. A full-fledged prayer this time. Evidently, her heart was beginning to open up to the idea of trusting in divine intervention like Rick did. How about that? Evidently, it was making the decision for her when she wasn't looking. She shrugged. *Let's see where this goes.*

She thought about Larry, Rick, and Chief Orbison up on the bridge. She was glad they were working this case with her. Especially Rick. He could be bossy like her dad. That was why she kept resisting the strong attraction between them. She could never live with the sort of dominance her mother did. Besides, their friendship and coworker interaction was something she relied on—to the point that she sometimes wondered how she managed to function all those years without him in her life. It worried her to rely so much on him, but she did not want to lose that either.

Larry's hail from above had her returning to the bridge. Orbison had cut the power back to idling speed and deployed the anchors to hold them in place as they studied the chart on the table.

"What's up, guys?"

"Accordin' ta our GPS," Orbison said, "we're 'bout twenty yards from the position where Blackstone's Cessna went down. Even with our shallow draft, we're as close as we can get with the *Mae*. From here, we hafta use somethin' else. Maybe the Zodiac."

"It's still too dark to do a visual, isn't it, Chief?" Rick kept glancing outside and back at the chart under the lighted binnacle.

"What about a lighted scuba tour?" Larry's question snapped

everyone's head toward him. "We might be able to find something that way. Just sayin'."

"He's more than an empty stomach, ain't he?" Orbison said.

"Now you see why we put up with him," Aims said. "He comes in pretty handy sometimes."

"So, exactly what are we looking for here? I want to know where my focus is." Larry's scarecrow mind was obviously operating at full power this morning.

"I thought we had two areas of focus," Aims replied. "Any other wreckage from Blackstone's plane and any evidence of what happened to Admiral Carter's aide, Bryce Wilford."

"Sounds right to me," Rick said. Orbison nodded his agreement as he turned to go aft to the dive station near the fantail and begin to prepare the equipment they would need.

"Good one," Rick said to Larry as he turned to help Orbison. "Let's you and I get suited up, Stringbean." Larry followed.

Light was beginning to streak the eastern sky while Rick and Larry scoured the grasses of the marshy area around the crash site. They kept up a running commentary on their throat mics, while Aims monitored their video feed and Orbison kept track of their dive status. An image flickered onto Aims's screen just as Rick muttered. "Oh, oh."

"What is that?" Aims asked. She had always known this moment would come, especially on plane crash cases. In the past, however, Rick had been right there with her to reach out a hand, to reassure her that he would walk with her through it. But this time, he was underwater and yards away from her. She was not sure she could do this without him. By herself, she didn't think she had the strength.

She felt bile rising in her throat, threatening a gag response. Who was going to help her?

In that moment, her mind began to play the words Rick often said to her when panic threatened. *Remember, Aims, God tells us to fear not, for He is with us. Don't be afraid, for He is our God. He promises to give us strength and help. He offers us His strong right hand.* Peace washed through her, and she could breathe again. In that moment, she felt God's presence like she had not experienced in years. At the same time, she felt a new closeness to Rick. The fog in her mind cleared, and she could hear Rick and Larry talking to her.

"It's a foot. Got a body attached. We have pictures and GPS location?" Larry was asking.

"Yeah," she said. "Just downloaded all that to our hard drive now. Larry, launch a marker buoy. I'll be right there with the Zodiac. Have we found Captain Wilford?"

"Looks like it. It's the right uniform. Wait one."

Aims paused at the monitor station, watching the video feed. The camera panned over the image of a body lying facedown, wearing a navy captain's uniform. It still had the parachute harness strapped to it. The image zoomed in to the harness and showed that the parachute shroud lines were cut cleanly where they joined the harness.

"Rick," she said, "is the canopy nearby? Any sign of the admiral's briefcase? Do you think Wilford hit some part of the plane on his way out?"

"Don't think so. We need to widen our search radius to be sure."

"Okay. Why don't you and Larry roll him? Let's get a look at his front."

"That was next. Here we go." The two divers rolled the body while their headlamps illuminated the video feed.

"Whoa," Aims said. "That's a horror mask if I've ever seen one. Our Captain Wilford was not very happy with the last thing he saw."

"I'd say the sight of an incoming .22-caliber bullet could be part of the reason for that. We got a small GSW in the left temple to match those of the pilot and admiral on the plane. Unless he was a southpaw, I'd rule out suicide."

"I agree," Aims replied. "Seems like every piece of evidence we uncover raises more questions. Now we have a missing briefcase, murder weapon, and parachute canopy. We don't know what was in the briefcase or who brought down the plane, except for White's report of a fireball and the missile launch tube."

"Yeah, well," Rick said, "we'll just keep looking. Sometimes you just have to keep beating the bushes and see what comes out."

"Okay," Aims said. "Then we will. I'm coming to get you guys with the Zodiac."

Orbison helped Aims launch the Zodiac and took over communications with the team while the three of them wrestled the waterlogged body into the inflatable boat. Rick climbed in first to help Aims steady the craft and receive Wilford's body.

"Sorry I couldn't get to you when you first realized we had a dead body," he said. He gently touched Aims's shoulder.

"It's okay," she replied. "I received some help from an unexpected source."

When Rick's eyebrows rose, she said, "Tell you about it later. Let's get Wilford on board." With Larry using the buoyancy of the water to help, they finished loading the body and motored back to the *Maisie Mae*. By now, there was enough daylight to see what they were doing. Rick and Larry shucked out of their tanks and shed their flippers, and Larry began taking more photos of Wilford's body. Orbison stowed the Zodiac and their gear, and Aims made contact with Brunswick. They emailed the photos and coordinates where the body was found.

All of that time, Rick kept an eye on Aims. There was a new strength in her mannerisms that had him wondering about where that unexpected assistance had come from. As his curiosity grew, he knew that he would be cornering her at the first chance that presented itself.

"Are you bringing him back now?" Collier asked Rick when Aims finished her initial report.

"We've only just begun our investigation here, sir," Rick replied. "We haven't had a chance to talk to Blackstone or find out who brought the plane down. We've got a missing briefcase, whose contents are unknown, a missing parachute canopy, and a missing murder weapon. We're going to need most of this day and I don't know how many more to see if we can find all these things. But we need to get the ME's report on Wilford ASAP too. Can we get another ferry flight from the Marco Island airport?"

"I've got a better idea," Collier replied. "I'll contact the Coast Guard station at Fort Meyers Beach to send a search-and-rescue chopper to your location. They can lift the body aboard and bring it back here, and you won't have to leave your search area. How does that sound?"

"Good," Rick replied. "Our taxi driver agrees."

"How is that working out?"

"Great. We got the red tape taken care of, didn't we?"

"Yeah," Collier said. "Helps to have the SECNAV in your corner. The Coasties will contact you with their ETA. Happy hunting."

"You get all that, Chief?"

"Yup. I got some buddies at Fort Meyers. I'm activatin' my locator beacon on their frequency so they'll know where we are." Orbison activated the beacon and raised the anchor, and they began a slow troll of the marshy area, hoping to find the location from which the missile was launched at Blackstone's plane. The team put binoculars to their eyes and began scanning preassigned quadrants while Orbison navigated from his charts.

A short time later, Aims heard the telltale whop-whop of helicopter rotors signaling the arrival of the Coast Guard. Orbison and the helicopter crew orchestrated the descent of the body stretcher and its return to the hovering aircraft. The investigators were unhappy with the noisy operation and the possible loss of any element surprise, but it was necessary one. They could only grit their teeth and continue searching. As Rick had said, there were a lot of bushes to be beaten, and they were not even sure there would be anything there to find. All in the day's work for investigators.

The sun reached its zenith over the coastal islands; the team had been searching the grids they had laid out for hours. Aims had rotated onto the dive team and off again. The other two took regular shifts, switching off to prevent nitrogen buildup in the blood. Now, Orbison set out an array of cold cuts for sandwiches. He had rigged a large glass container between the solar panels, and it had been brewing sun tea. He put out anchors, fore and aft, so that they could continue their grid search after they ate. The underwater sonar surveillance system and radar antennae continued to turn. Now was not the time to relax their vigilance.

When they had finished eating, Orbison said, "Well, this mornin's had a mixed review."

"Yeah," Larry said. "I feel like all we have done is scratch off empty squares of the grid."

"We did find Wilford," Aims observed. "No telling what the ME will have to say about him."

"There's that," Orbison said. "While y'all've have been snorkelin' around, enjoyin' the swimming, I been looking at the charts."

"I think I hear the approach of some fascinating words of wisdom," Rick said, his gaze focusing on Orbison.

"I don't know if it occurred to any of y'all," Orbison began. "But when a county resident buys property and it's placed on the tax rolls, the legal description is posted on all the county maps. Any agency that might hafta provide any public services knows about it. In the case of buying a private island, the Coast Guard is also notified, lest the owners need of any of their services too.

"Both the fire and rescue crews as well as the Coast Guard are given regular updates. This grid search that we been doin' is leadin' us toward Obsidian Haven."

"And that would be ..." Rick began.

"That's Blackstone's private fishing retreat, isn't it?" Aims said.

"I bet you're a killer with logic problems." Orbison was grinning in appreciation.

"I get it," Larry said. "Obsidian is a black stone."

"Two points for Stringbean too." Rick laughed.

"Let's take a look at the island on the chart and get an idea what we're talking about," Aims suggested. "I think I want a clear picture of the geography involved before we make any moves."

Orbison was already on the move toward the binnacle on the

bridge, and Aims cleared the table so they could spread out the chart and gather around it.

According to information from the Coast Guard, Obsidian Haven was a roughly kidney bean–shaped island that lay at the end of a meandering passage between low, uninhabited islands. These functioned as a sort of barrier between it and the open water of the Gulf of Mexico. They suggested a protection for the island during tropical storms, lessening a large portion of any damage to the structures on the island. It was roughly four miles in length and approximately two and a half miles at its widest point. The slight inward curve that faced the passage from the Gulf invited the presence of a main house. Blackstone had obviously accepted that invitation and had added some surrounding cabanas for guests. A long dock was marked on the chart, suggesting the location where Blackstone's yacht, the *Obsidian*, would be secured. The landward side of the island indicated the presence of more small islands, which were also marked as uninhabited.

"What sort of vegetation is on these islands?" Rick asked. "Is it like what we're seeing on these islands around us?"

"Pretty much," Orbison replied. "Mangrove, palmetto, and sea grape. Saw grass and occasional low coconut palms. Tropical storms during the summer keep 'em low. Sea birds like ta nest in the lower levels, but they hafta be on the lookout for snakes and alligators, who love the eggs. Sort of a delicate balance."

"Sea grapes seem to be the most beneficial for limiting sight lines between the islands," Larry observed. "Make good hunting blinds."

"Ya noticed that too, did ya?" Orbison chuckled. "Where'd ya do your huntin'?"

"Florida Panhandle, sir," Larry replied. "My daddy got us season licenses for bear and deer, and we hunted with both longbow and rifles. Razorback hogs too."

"You've been holding out on us, Larry," Aims observed. "I never would have pegged you for a hunter."

"Never came up, Skipper." Larry grinned.

"Okay, y'all," Orbison said, bringing their attention back to the charts. "Here's where we been searchin', and as I mentioned before, y'all'll see that the grids drift toward Blackstone's Obsidian Haven. Do you wanna continue that?"

"Well, Chief," Rick began, "what were you going to suggest as our next search route?"

Just then, the laptop in front of Aims chimed, signaling incoming communication for the team. She looked at the size of the attachments to the email and looked up at Orbison.

"How secure are we in this location right now?" she asked him.

"Well," he said slowly, "there's been no sign of a threat. Looks like we're not gonna find any evidence other than the body that's already gone to your ME. So, I'd say we're probably as secure here as anywhere. Why?"

"The messages incoming as attachments to an email from our office indicate that we're getting several large chunks of info. They'll take some chewing on in order to digest them. I think we'd be better off taking some time now and going through them before we go any further."

Rick came around to stand behind her, checking to see what the attachments could be.

"Wow," he said. "Looks like Collier had the whole crew on all-nighters to get that amount of info to us so quickly. I think you're right, Aims. As long as we're secure here, this is the time and place to see what we've got so we can make good plans for our next step."

"Y'all can forward these to the big screen in the salon," Orbison said. "That way, we can all read the reports at the same time.

Chapter 5

The first dossier that came up was for Captain Bryce Wilford, who was still a missing person at the time that Brunswick began compiling their report. As the information about his family showed up, Aims spoke.

"I thought that name sounded familiar. There was a Stephen Wilford a couple of years ahead of me at Annapolis. He was a real star. Best quarterback Navy has had in recent years. In fact, since Roger Staubach. Some said he was even better. Not only did he have a better record than Staubach, but the academic people said he was even smarter. Aced all his strategic studies and never lost a war game assigned to him and his group. His record at the Top Gun school was legendary, and his was the only aircraft to be shot down by enemy aircraft in the Gulf War. They said it took three aircraft ganging up on him to do it, and he took two of them with him.

"This Bryce must have been his little brother. When I was finishing fighter pilot training, the instructors were talking about Steve Wilford's little brother's lackluster performance at Annapolis."

"This information," Rick began, "says he was a cee-level sailor.

Finished in the bottom third of his class and washed out of flight school."

"Younger siblings of star performers get lotsa expectations hung on them," Orbison said. "If they can't come up ta the mark o' of their older sibling, things get really tough. Navy instructors and NCOs talk. The grapevine's full o' reputations ruined because o' the scuttlebutt."

"Says here," Larry said, "he washed out of SEAL training as well. Here's a FITREP that says Bryce tried to 'skate on his big brother's reputation but couldn't cut it. Did not take reprimands and consequences well.'"

"So, how did he get assigned to a Pentagon post as Admiral Carter's aide?" Rick was literally scratching his head.

Aims was speed-reading through the background information, and after a moment, she replied to his question.

"Their dad was also an alumnus of Annapolis and a huge fan of Navy football. Not only that. He made a fortune as a defense contractor and had a lot of influence on Capitol Hill. He bought that assignment for Bryce, looks like. It was not earned, from the looks of his record."

"Well, then, let's look at the admiral. What was his assignment at the Pentagon, and what kind of information did Wilford have access to as his aide?" Larry was manipulating the feed from laptop to plasma as he spoke. "I don't have a problem with Daddy buying Sonny a job," he continued as Admiral James Carter's dossier came up. "As long as he didn't open the door to the treasure chest of military secrets."

They watched as the dossier of Admiral Carter came up on

the big screen. By tacit agreement, they skipped the biographical information and went to his current assignment.

"Okay," said Rick. "Office of Procurement. That can be pretty benign, can't it?"

"Yeah," Orbison commented. "Who cares about the supplier o' toilet paper and paper towels?"

"Oh, oh. This could be trouble," Rick said. "'Monitoring performance of hardware and software at interface with global positioning satellites for guidance and targeting of drones, missiles, and other smart ammunition.' What does that mean, Larry? And in English, please."

"Right, boss. Well, remember when we first started using smart bombs?" At Rick's nod, Larry continued. "Well, remember that there had to be someone on the ground, with line of sight to the target, and had to aim a laser targeting marker for the bomb or missile to lock onto, and it had to be held there for the entire descent of the weapon onto the target?"

"Yeah," Rick said. "There were a couple of occasions while I was on sniper duty in Afghanistan, when I had to be the someone on the ground holding the laser beam onto the target. It could get a little hairy. Then my tour was up, and was I glad."

"I would think so," Larry agreed. "Anyway, do you remember how, not too long ago, we began using drones for targeting smart weapons so there wouldn't have to be someone on the ground to hold the target beam in place?"

"Yeah, so?" Rick said.

"Well, then, instead of having to have the drone pilots in the area of the target, we began to be able to control them remotely, even from here in the States. And instead of having to have actual aircraft pilots do the controlling, kids who were aces at the arcades on war game machines could do it just as well. We didn't need the expense of training fighter pilots to control the drones, and we didn't have to pay hazard pay bonuses to these young guys. They had already been training themselves in the game arcades and at home with their game boxes. And some of them were pretty good, not only at controlling the drone but evading detection and being shot at."

"Even I am followin' that," Orbison commented. "But ... I hear a *but* comin'."

"Yes," Larry said. "There's a but. Essentially, the military was using game box technology for all of this. That's when Blackstone came along. His company, the Onyx Group—oh, okay, another black stone—offered the military a package of hardware and software that could be installed and would communicate with the GPS system, the command nodule, and the weapon in question to form a secure, discreet network to take the guesswork out of the guidance and targeting process. At the onset of the mission, the drones' coordinates were programmed into the onboard computer, and the command nodules' were programmed into the guidance computer. During the flight to target, the GPS was kept up to date on the weapon's position, which was then communicated to the controller. The guy with the game box then made whatever corrections needed to be made in order to be sure that the weapon hit the target.

"Now, here's the but. A lot of the control was put in the hands of the GPS and its computers."

"And when the control is split between the GPS and the military command nodules, it becomes like a weak spot in the chain of command," Aims said. "Huge but."

"Right," Larry agreed.

"How do you know all this?" Rick said.

"I'm a gamer in my spare time, boss," Larry said with a grin. "In fact, I was contacted a year or so ago to see if I wanted to become a drone pilot. But I decided I like what I'm doing with you guys, so I politely declined."

"And," Aims continued, bringing them back on point, "as with any military defense contract, the Pentagon has some guy in an office who can understand what the provided item was supposed to do and monitor what it actually did. That guy reports that to the secretary of defense. That was Carter's job."

"So," Rick said, staring at the screen, "Carter has been looking over Blackstone's shoulder. Do we think he found something wrong with the performance data?"

"Did we not see the recent news reports of civilian casualties and missed military targets?" Aims responded.

"When we found Carter's body," she said, "did we find a cell phone?"

She was already flipping through her notes of their check-in with Brunswick last night. "Yes, we did, and we sent it along with the bodies and wreckage of the plane. We'll need to get the office geeks to look into his phone records and see if he sent any hint of what he was finding to Blackstone."

"What about Wilford?" Rick said. "We didn't send a cell phone back with him, did we?"

"No," said Larry. "I checked his pockets while we were waiting for the Coast Guard pickup."

"We left a marker buoy where we found the body, didn't we, Larry?"

"Yes, boss, we did."

Orbison said, "Let's go on back there an' have us another look-see. Maybe Wilford spilled the beans ta Blackstone. Or maybe White. We can get a record of it off his cell phone."

"We'll also need to get phone records for Blackstone and White. Do we have a tame federal judge who would grant a warrant for us?" Aims was thinking a couple of steps ahead, something that Rick relied on her for.

"First, Aims," he said, "let's see what we can come up with from this end before we step outside of our little circle."

"You're right," she said. "Okay. What's next?"

"Let's get back to where we found Wilford," Rick said. "We still have a couple hours of daylight, and maybe we can come up with his cell phone."

Orbison was already headed to the bridge to move the *Maisie Mae*, and Larry and Rick were headed for the dive station on the fantail to suit up.

Aims moved to the monitoring station as the *Mae's* engines rumbled to life and the boat moved back toward their marker buoy.

After a couple of hours, Larry broke the surface, one arm high in the air.

"Got it, Skipper!" His hand clutched the sought-after prize.

Just then, Orbison and Aims heard a loud buzzing approaching overhead. They looked up to see a boxy object topped with small, whirling rotors and spitting bullets into the water as it approached the marker buoy.

"Down, Larry!" Aims yelled, reaching for her sidearm. She only got one shot off at the contraption before it broke off and headed back toward the Gulf of Mexico.

Aims had her cell phone out while the sound of the drone's engines could still be heard.

When the Brunswick office came on the line, she said, "Sir, can you get a military satellite feed of our coordinates? What are they, Chief?"

When Orbison read them off, she repeated them into her phone.

"Why do you want this, Aims?" her boss asked.

"We have just had an attack by drone, and I want to know if you can locate its control nodule," she replied. She turned to Orbison. "Get those guys out of the water and under cover, Chief. Let's get out of here in case they come back."

"Yes, ma'am," Orbison replied, a satisfied smile playing across his mouth. *She's still a good navy officer* was his thought. He signaled to the divers.

"Y'all okay?"

"Yeah," Rick said into his microphone. "Were those bullets in the water?"

"You betcha. Armed drone. Commander says return to base. Bring the marker buoy with ya. Meet y'all at the dive station. Commander says we're movin' out of here. And I got a plan B ready for us."

When Rick and Larry arrived at the dive station, they handed up the marker buoy before pulling themselves up onto the platform.

"Go ahead, Chief," Rick said. "We'll take care of the rest of this while you get us out of here."

"Okay," Orbison said. "But you guys grab ahold of something. This thing'll take off like a rocket. It's too dark ta come back and look for a man overboard."

"Gotcha," Rick and Larry said. "Go for it, Chief. We'll be okay."

Orbison stowed the marker buoy on his way to the enclosed bridge. "Hang on, Commander," he said, donning night vision goggles. "She takes off fast when I open 'er up."

"Aye, Chief," Aims replied. "Let 'er rip."

True to his word, Orbison opened the throttle levers that looked to Aims like throttles on an aircraft. The quickly responding boat practically buried its stern in the water as the nose came up, and the boat became the tip of an arrow of wake widening behind them.

Rick and Larry managed to stow their dive gear while maintaining their hold on the rail. When they were dressed in dry clothing, they joined Aims and Orbison on the bridge. Aims was watching the radar screen, and Rick noticed that they were running dark. The only illumination anywhere on the *Maisie Mae* were the red battle lamps in the bridge enclosure. Rick and Larry had just stepped inside when a low island appeared on Aims's screen. In addition to the usual tropical foliage, there was a large boxlike structure that extended a good distance into the surrounding water. Orbison cut the power back, and the prow settled into the water as their speed dropped dramatically. He touched a button on the console, and the boxy image virtually disappeared. He let the *Mae* coast toward where they had seen the structure, and they realized they were entering a huge boathouse. As soon as their stern was inside, Orbison touched the button on the console again, and the overhead door descended. Only then did he power up the illumination inside.

The team of investigators looked around in amazement. Although there was only one other craft moored inside, there was room enough for several. Orbison pulled their boat close to the catwalk along the left side of the structure.

"Get the lines, will ya, Rick?" Orbison asked.

"Sure, Chief," Rick said. "Larry, secure the stern, okay?"

Both men jumped across the narrow gap of water, grabbed the coiled lines, and secured the *Maisie Mae* against the used tires acting as dock bumpers. When they were back on board the *Mae*, Orbison doused the lighting of the boathouse and turned on the interior lighting of their craft.

"Okay, Chief," Rick said, "what exactly is plan B?"

"And where are we?" Larry asked. "I mean, whose boathouse is this? Looks like a maritime parking lot, with only one car here besides us."

Orbison grinned.

"My buddy's in the Coast Guard at Station Fort Meyers. Him 'n' me own this place and the island it sits on. There've been times in the past when we needed a place ta run to when things got dicey. Besides that, we take derelict boats and turn them into somethin' better. I rebuilt the *Lindy Lou* here. The *Mae* too. The only one car besides us, as you called her, is also one o' our joint creations."

The three investigators looked out the windows of the salon at the odd-looking craft sharing their parking lot.

"What is that craft, Chief?" Rick asked. "I spent a lot of years building and rebuilding boats with my uncle in Baton Rouge. I thought I had seen every sort of boat made, but that one doesn't fit any one category. Looks kind of like a patchwork quilt."

"Good eye, marine," Orbison said. "That's sorta what it is.

"My buddy and I were brainstormin' one night over pizza and coffee and asked ourselves some what-if questions."

Aims had been staring at the other craft all this time. "Like, what if a cruiser could be converted into a sailboat and back again?

If someone was looking for a cruiser, they'd ignore the sloop-rigged sailboat, right?"

Orbison nodded. "Right on, Commander. Sharp lady you are."

"The paint job has me scratching my head," Larry said. "Exactly what color is that thing?"

"I didn't know they were making those changeable color paints for marine craft," Rick said. "I mean, we've seen some of them on customized street stock race cars, but I've never heard of them for marine use."

"Only been on the market for a year or so. If you're gonna hide a boat in plain sight, why not create some confusion as ta what color it is?" Orbison was watching their faces as they listened to him.

"What's your Coastie buddy's name?" Larry asked. "You guys are so sneaky, and I want to be able to keep an eye on you two. You'd be walking crime sprees if you ever went off the reservation."

"He's no problem." Orbison chuckled. "And his name, believe it or not, is Davy Jones."

"Okay, Chief," Aims said. "Tell us about your quilt over there. Since the bad guys have seen our boat, is that what we're going to be riding in when we leave here? And when will that be? Is this where we spend the night? I'm interested in the shape of this plan B of yours."

"Yes, ma'am," Orbison responded. "That's a rough sketch. We can do whatever modifications y'all think we need.

"We spend the night here. Yes, we'll have to leave the *Maisie Mae* here since she's come into the crosshairs of our hunters. As your security consultant, I think you should leave your laptop and cell phones here. When we transfer to the *Chameleon*, we'll have new burn phones and a clean laptop to plug into the military encrypted communications network. If they're hackin' us, they won't be able ta read our mail.

"The *Chameleon* has the same power plant as a Coast Guard cutter, so she can do both pursuit and evasion. She has a retractable counter board for when she's under sail, and her mast can be carried as deck cargo. We put it into place when we need to. She's a true convertible."

"Who drew up her plans?" Rick asked. "I want one of those when I grow up."

The laughter was therapeutic for all of them.

"So," Orbison continued, "what do y'all think about my plan B? Do we need any changes?"

"Do you have the clean electronics here?" Rick asked.

"We got a small emergency supply depot here. The *Chameleon* is already fueled and ready to sail. We transfer our belongings and food supplies next. If you like the plan, we should make the transfer right away and get plugged into the communications network ASAP. That way, any info that comes from your home office will be at hand when you might need it. We leave when the tide turns in the early morning. We don't wanna be seen comin' outa our parkin' lot."

The navy investigators packed their few personal belongings, including removing the batteries from their cell phones and laptop and stowing them away in their staterooms before transferring to the *Chameleon* across the waterway. Orbison packed the food and other provisions and set them out for the others to transfer along with their personal gear. Then, like any conscientious yachtsman, he shut down systems aboard the *Maisie Mae* so she would be secure and ready for use when they came back to her.

After the transfer, Aims and the team explored their new

transport, marveling at what Orbison and Jones had been able to fit into the compact space. Every convenience that had been available to them aboard the *Mae* was included here. They had access to diving gear and electronic security measures for both surface and underwater surveillance. The communications provisions rivalled the secure center at Brunswick. Orbison had raided the supply depot in the boathouse, and not only did they have clean cell phones and laptop, they also had a small arsenal and ammunition in case of attack. Rick and Aims were astounded to find a setup for antisubmarine warfare, as well as missile defense technology and measures. These guys hadn't missed a trick.

"I wonder who they thought they were going to be facing," Aims murmured to Rick.

"I don't think I want to know," he replied.

The team discussed what they needed to be doing.

"You know, boss," Larry began, "while I was downloading our laptop's files on this case onto a flash drive, it occurred to me that when the bad guys fired off that missile, they burned any vegetation that was behind them with the back flame. If a satellite had infrared imaging capability, they still might be able to pinpoint the exact location if we gave them the coordinates of where we found the launch tube. Finding that and taking pictures of it would be helpful in building our case against them when we have located them and are charging them."

"That's good, Larry," Aims said. "It might show up better if they did the looking at night when the surrounding water and vegetation were cooler. What I'm thinking is getting that request to the NRO right away. If they locate the area and take infrared photos of the area, that is one task we can mark off our list, and we won't have to backtrack."

Orbison looked over at Rick. "I can see why ya keep 'em around, marine," he said.

"Yeah. Handy, aren't they? You're saying, Aims," he continued to her, "that after the visit to the *Obsidian,* the next item on our agenda is probably finding the base camp for the guys who brought down the plane. Right?"

"I think so. I'm just concerned about keeping the *Chameleon* off everybody's radar as long as possible.

"We were thinking about Wilford's parachute canopy, but I think that can wait for a while. We need Admiral Carter's briefcase to know what he was concerned about, and we also need the murder weapon. Finding the shooters would be good because we might be able to link them to Blackstone and White.

"You know, the more I think about it, the more I'm thinking that Blackstone may be not much more than an unwitting dupe to White's schemes. What do you think about that, Chief?"

"Inclined to agree with ya," Orbison said. "It's always been my impression of Blackstone … maybe White. As for the list of evidence we still need, that's above my pay grade. More in your wheelhouse than mine. As far as keeping the *Chameleon* off the radar, that's not a problem. We got a longboat that'll get ya ta either the island or the yacht while *Chameleon* stays out of sight over the horizon.

"I agree, finding the base camp and questioning Blackstone and White should be our next projects. We can plug in our request to the NRO right away. Then we can set our watch schedule until the tide turns. We leave as a cruiser first to put as much distance between us and the boathouse as we can before first light. By the time the sun is up, I want us rigged for sail as a sloop and looking as harmless as warm milk."

"I like your plan B, Chief." Rick said. "Let's do it."

Aims closed the door of her stateroom and eyed the compact quarters. Another night in a strange bed with unfamiliar surroundings, and another day of tension and adrenaline to be quelled so she could try to get some sleep. Tomorrow promised to be another long and stressful day. She wondered how many more of these she could subject herself to before her body or mind rebelled permanently. Not to be considered. *Get over it, Aims. You signed on for this job, so take a deep breath and do it.* It wasn't like she was the only one dealing with these pressures. The whole team, including Orbison, was facing the same thing. *Wonder how many of these Orbison has coped with over the years.* Now that was something to think about. *If he can deal with it, then so can you. Don't be a wuss. Remember, God is with us.*

With a sigh of resignation, Aims dropped her head onto the pillow and closed her eyes. Rick's face swam onto her mental screen. His smile. The affection and caring in his eyes. His prayers for her when she lay helpless in the hospital. His steadfast faith when hers was nonexistent. How had she even survived? What would have happened to her if he had not showed up at the hospital? She knew he cared for her. Why was he still single? Why was he still hanging around her when she gave him no hope that their relationship would be any different than it was right now? And what about the recent involuntary responses to his touch? Did they signal some sort of change that her heart was undergoing? A decision it was making for her? Was God taking part in this process? The weariness finally overcame her, leaving the questions still circling, still waiting to be answered, to be faced again at some other time. She slept.

❦ ⊷❀⊶ ❦

Rick lay staring into the darkness. He waited for the tension to ease away from his body and mind. His thoughts wanted to swirl in his head, but he knew coherent thought was out of the question. Among them was the difference in Aims's responses to him. What did that mean? As he often did when faced with a short night and a dangerous, complex problem, he lifted a prayer. *Can't deal with any of this, Lord. I need Your peace, Your assurance that You know and are handling all of this. And all of us. Take care of us and all of this while we rest. Thank You.*

Chapter 6

When the sun rose the next morning out of the eastern Caribbean, the sea was calm, nearly glassy. Its reflection of the sunrise painted the water with rich colors before the sky turned to blue and the sun was a huge gold disc. Orbison was taking the morning watch as the sloop-rigged yacht ghosted along under the fore sail. The *Chameleon* looked like an ad for a yachting magazine, picture-perfect, with a beautiful woman in a stylish swimsuit standing in the prow and two fit, younger men helping the boat's captain with the sail and lines while enjoying the caress of the breeze caused by the boat's passage.

NRO had responded to their request before they had even set the evening watch, and with the *Chameleon* still in cruiser mode, they had motored by the location, of which they had been provided infrared photos. Of course, the shooters were long gone, and the only evidence of their presence was the flattened reeds wearing the scorch marks of the missile's backfire. As the team had suspected, the area where they found the launch tube was on the way out of the maze of marshy terrain where the plane went down. A look at the charts indicated that the plane's attackers had probably headed into the vicinity of Obsidian Haven Island.

Now they were establishing an innocent presence for all to see in the Gulf, away from coastal boat traffic. At the same time, Orbison was taking them to a position that would disguise the point of origin of their longboat's visit to Blackstone's Obsidian Haven. Brunswick was still looking into the backgrounds of White's list of employees, and they were examining the bodies and wreckage of the plane crash as well.

"Gonna take several hours before we git ta the spot I want us ta be at," Orbison had said. The boat was under sail; therefore, they had a limited rate of travel. Aims was grateful for a little bit of downtime. They had been dealing with crises nonstop since being shot at while at the fire station immediately after their arrival in Naples.

Aims turned toward the stern of the boat and watched the sea and sky brighten with the day. It should have been time to reflect on the peace of the scene, but Aims could not forget that it had been during just such routine information gathering that the two direct attacks on the team had occurred. She figured it was not a good idea to let their guard down. How did their attackers know where to find them? Were they after the navy team or Orbison? Or both?

She watched Rick and Larry as they moved around the boat. Her attention centered on Rick, as it usually did, since the moment she opened her eyes to find him in the ICU with her after her fighter crash. There was something essential about his warmth and presence that nourished her. His faith had become as important to her as he was. She had begun lifting a prayer in difficult situations, like Rick did for her during her recovery. Here she was doing that now. *Dear Lord, I know that we haven't been on very good terms. I'm sorry that I haven't done a better job at this communication thing with You. Rick does this praying thing better than I do. But this situation has me scared. It looks like we're dealing with some heavy hitters here, and I don't have a clue how we're going to cope with that. Could You please give us some direction and maybe even some protection here? I'd really appreciate it.*

Aims turned back toward the west, looking off toward the Gulf of Mexico. She eased herself down, resting her back against the front wall of the main cabin between the windows. Resting her arms on her drawn-up knees, she began thinking about the upcoming interview with Blackstone. She knew that White had planned to accompany them to Obsidian's Haven, but she felt better that the plan now called for them to make their visit unannounced and unaccompanied by White.

She had only been watching the horizon for a few moments when Rick slid down onto the deck beside her. He handed her a steaming cup of coffee before taking a sip from his own mug.

"How are you?" He bumped her shoulder gently before settling back beside her against the forward bulkhead of the cabin. At his touch, a surge response coursed through her to her core. No denying it. Something different was going on. She wished she had time to explore it.

"Thanks for the coffee," she said. "I'm good. I'm thinking about C. Arthur Blackstone and our coming interview."

"Penny."

"Probably would be an overpayment."

"If it is," he said quietly, "it would be the first time."

"Hmmm. Thanks."

"So, what are you thinking?"

"I was thinking about who would be on board the *Obsidian*

with Blackstone and his family. Remember when I was questioning White? I asked him when Blackstone would be returning home. He said they would stay out the rest of the week."

"I recall that," Rick said. "I remember that White said that Blackstone was expecting more guests, and that was why the plane had gone to Connecticut to pick up Admiral Carter and Wilford. Evidently, whoever the guests already present were, they were perceived to be of enough importance to keep them out here."

"Carter was a three-star, wasn't he? Doesn't that put him pretty high on the food chain in the Procurement Office? I mean, doesn't his report on a contractor have a lot to do with whether the contractor keeps his contract or gets a new one?"

"It does."

"So, it would be beneficial to keep such a person pretty well satisfied, wouldn't it?"

"It would. A contractor with an unhappy procurement officer would have very few options, I'd say. Either make him happy again or get rid of him—that is, if he wants to keep doing business with the government. A third option, of course, would be to stop being a government contractor."

"But," Aims objected, "if most of your annual net profits are generated by government contracts, that third option would not look so appealing. Would it? I mean, you'd choose a course of action that would keep the money coming in, wouldn't you?"

"So, that brings you back to your original question. Who else is on the *Obsidian* who rates high enough with Blackstone to outrank the source of his annual net profits?"

"Remember when we were in training to be investigators?" Aims said, staring off toward the horizon. "They hammered us with one recurring axiom. Follow the money. Who profits? In this case, the question would be, who provides the most profits to Blackstone? He's savvy enough in business not to strangle one goose laying golden eggs unless he has another goose to lay some in the next nest. Who is that other goose?"

"He's skating on thin ice if he's blowing off the US government," Rick said. "With the possible exceptions of ISIS and their domestic terrorists, even other nations approach such a decision with some care. Blackstone's other goose better have some pretty hefty firepower behind her."

"So," Aims said, "literally, who in the world could that be? I think we should have an idea who that is before we set foot on the *Obsidian*. Going in fat, happy, and ignorant doesn't appeal."

"I agree," Rick said. "That wouldn't be smart. I think we should run these thoughts by Orbison. He might have an idea who some of Blackstone's recent pals might be. Once again, Aims, not an overpayment. Come on." Rick stood, reached for Aims's empty coffee mug, and headed aft to talk to Orbison. Aims motioned to Larry as they went through the salon, and both of them followed at his heels.

As the team edged into the now crowded bridge house, Orbison glanced up from the charts he was following.

"What's up? Y'all look serious."

"Chief," Rick began, "we've been discussing our approach to Blackstone and his passengers on the *Obsidian*. We agreed that it would be a good idea to know who we are likely to encounter there."

"And," Aims interjected, "we've been wondering about the fact that the plane crash was not important enough to Blackstone to cut his trip short and return to Marco Island to see to the details surrounding the deaths of his pilot and his influential guests from the Pentagon."

"Especially since present and future incomes are tied to the admiral?" Larry added.

"Wondered about that," Orbison said. "Is he about to shoot himself in the foot when it comes ta doin' business with the government?"

"For himself," Rick responded, "not if he has another customer with deeper pockets or better perks to take the government's place. But if you think about the national security picture, that might be extremely dangerous for all of us, as well as for him and his family."

"'Cause whoever he could be courtin' has got no qualms about killin' a high-rankin' admiral or takin' on the US government," Orbison said, staring off into space.

"We were wondering if Blackstone has been entertaining visitors who could fit that description," Aims said. "Do you have any way to know or find out about that?"

"Funny ya should ask that," Orbison said, scowling. "'Member I said I thought Maisie's choice of male companions showed poor judgment?" When the team all nodded, Orbison continued. "Well, this latest flame is a smooth-talkin' salesman for a golf equipment manufacturer. He's also a wannabe pro golfer and sometime caddy and pro at Mrs. Blackstone's golf club.

"He's a loud mouth an' a name-dropper. Lately, he's been braggin' about Mrs. Blackstone's guests that he's been caddyin' and providin' golf lessons for."

"And," Aims said, "who might they be?"

"Slick Sam, as I call him, has recently been snickering about Lady Blackstone's frolickin' with the handsome twin sons of a guy from some Arab country. Seems Daddy's supposed to be considerin' investin' in her husband's company. He guesses that she's on the shady side of forty, and they're crossin' the hump of their twenties."

"And he knows about this, how?" Rick asked.

"Well, Blackstone's been payin' for golf lessons for the two at her club. Sam's the part-time pro there. He's had a ringside seat to the goin's-on every day for the last week."

"We're going to need the specific information you have about this family, their exact surname, and the name of the Arab nation they're from, so we can dig into their backgrounds," Aims said. "Larry, you get that. Chief, we're going to need some time to do this digging, as well as alert Brunswick about this direction of our investigation."

After their conversation, Orbison furled the sail and dropped anchor. He stowed the sail and stepped the mast before settling into the fisherman's fighting chair with a pole and fishing line nestled in the holder in front of him. On his earlier tour of the *Chameleon*, he had revealed to the team that that particular pole holder was wired to be part of a network connecting the yacht with the secure and encrypted military communications satellite that served the tropical zone from the Canary Islands on the east to the Galapagos on the west. The fishing rod was a fiber optic antenna that received the satellite's signal for the yacht's local area network. The team gathered around the communications station, doing some of their own research after the heads-up to the home office. This strategy had the advantage of allowing them immediate access to the Skype call that came less than an hour later. The team gathered around the webcam to see the SECNAV's face.

"Good afternoon, agents."

"Good afternoon, sir," Rick responded. "What do you have for us?"

"First, I want to say good job on your investigation so far. I'm glad that you are working with Chief Orbison. I've found him extremely valuable over the years."

"Yes, sir. And he's continuing to be extremely valuable now."

"That being said," Johnson continued, "I'm sending to your laptops there a list of some of Admiral Carter's recent inquiries and the documents that they generated. All of that information was in the missing briefcase. We know that because Carter always left a list of documents that he had with him on his trips. And he did this time as well."

"Why did he do that?" Larry asked.

"Agent Robb," Johnson replied, "not everyone in the navy drives a boat. Someone has to keep track of the fuel in the tanks, the planes on the carriers, how efficient the personnel are, and the food in the galley. Admiral Carter was good at that kind of record keeping, and *that's* why he had the job in the Procurement Office. He always went by the book.

"Not only that, but he never made a negative report on anything or anybody without first checking it out for himself. That was why he was going to see Blackstone in person."

"Did you know why he wanted to talk to Blackstone?" Aims asked.

"Not before he left," Johnson said. "But I looked at what he had in his briefcase before I sent it to you. Confronting Blackstone in person was typical of the way he operated.

"Have you interviewed C. Arthur Blackstone yet?"

"No, sir," Rick said. "We sent a heads-up to Assistant Director

Collier in Brunswick an hour ago, saying that we wanted to do some research on who else we would likely encounter on his yacht before we made an appearance there."

"Was this information provided by his driver?"

"No, sir. As a matter of fact, Orbison himself provided that information."

"Now, how would he know that?" SECNAV's eyebrows took a sudden trip upward.

"Let's put it this way," Aims said. "Even a daughter's unwelcome suitor can have his uses."

Admiral Johnson groaned. "Oh, Commander Wallace," he said. "Don't make me go there. My daughter is just entering the dating phase." When the team chuckled, he showed a scowl. "Not funny, team.

"Anyway," he went on. "What did he have to offer?"

"Blackstone is hosting a family from an Arabian kingdom," Aims said. "We have been searching the internet for background information about them. The patriarch is a member of the royal family, but we're still trying to obtain specific information about him and his family. The local gossip is that the twin sons have graduate degrees from MIT, and Dad is interested in investing in Blackstone's Onyx Group.

"He has those twenty-something twin boys with him, and Orbison's daughter's boyfriend has been giving Blackstone's wife and the young bucks golf lessons. They are Ahmad and Anwar, and the family surname is Al Masih. Their graduate degrees are in cyber-electronic engineering."

"If Daddy is ready to invest in Onyx, we need more information before we know what implications that might have for national security issues." Rick was scowling by the time he finished that sentence. "At any rate, I think it is a good idea to complete this research before we venture into Blackstone's lion's den."

"I agree," SECNAV said. "You guys have had enough excitement out there. No need to take anything for granted. Your boss in Brunswick will be keeping me in the loop. I understand you've changed your transport after the drone attack yesterday. Keep watching your six."

"We will, sir." Aims and Larry nodded their agreement with Rick's acknowledgment.

"So, are you going to wait until tomorrow for the approach to Blackstone's party?"

"It would probably be a good idea if we did," Rick said. "Unless we have some unwanted visitors or run into any opposition in the meantime."

"Good. Let your boss, Collier, update me, unless you need more information that I can help you get."

"Aye, sir," Rick said as the communication link was terminated.

"Okay, team. Let's take a look at Carter's documents."

Larry put the documents provided by Admiral Johnson up on the plasma screen, and they began to look at them.

"Larry," Aims said, "how about arranging them in chronological order? That might give us an idea of Carter's thought process."

"Good idea, Aims," Rick said. "Can you do that, Larry?"

Larry spent a moment dragging the documents around until they had a starting date about six months ago, leading up to the previous week.

"Okay," said Aims, reading aloud, "the first one is a report on a drone strike aimed at a verified terrorist stronghold in the mountains of Iraq. The command nodule on board the carrier that launched it somehow lost control of it close to Amman, Jordan. That's when it veered off course, and instead of launching its missile, it crashed and struck a refugee camp, causing a lot of civilian casualties. The investigation by the navy could find no evidence of error on the part of the drone controllers, and they forwarded a request to the Pentagon for an investigation by the contractor for the targeting component, which happened to be the Onyx Group. They included the controller inputs and computer code to help identify whatever errors might have been present.

"Onyx got the request and waited six weeks to respond. Then they reported to the Pentagon Procurement Office that the component had functioned according to design. The failure was, quote, 'obviously an unreported operator targeting error.'

"The rest of the documents appear to be repeats of the original complaint and responses, for subsequent incidents. The final communication is from Admiral Carter to Blackstone. He asks for a face-to-face to clear up the confusion. It's dated three days before the plane crash."

"That's what?" Rick said. "One, two, three, four, five failures in twenty separate incidents, from three different command nodules?"

"Right," Larry responded.

"Were all the targeting components from the Onyx Group?" Rick was trying to determine the answer to his own question from the paperwork on display.

"According to Carter's research?" Aims said. "Yes. Wow, that's a 25 percent failure rate. That's either shoddy production quality control or deliberate sabotage, I'd say."

"In a nutshell," Rick growled.

"Where's Wilford phone?" Aims asked. "What's the call history on that phone?"

"I had it drying in a bowl of rice overnight," Larry said. "I didn't want to try to power it up until it's really dry inside. I'll go get it."

When he returned to his seat, Larry laid the now dry cell phone beside the laptop. "Okay," Larry said. "Since Blackstone knew about this, it seems like he might have done some pretty serious bridge burning."

"Let's see who Bryce Wilford has been calling and what he has been saying," Rick said.

Larry plugged the USB cable into the cell phone and connected it to their laptop, then put the images up on the plasma so they could all view what they found.

"Wow," Larry said. "This guy is a serious gaming addict. Takes one to know one. I haven't even reached that level on this game, and I'm a pretty good player."

"His need for porn seems to be pretty serious too," Rick observed. "Looks like his American Express card—he doesn't leave home without it."

"I'll say," Larry agreed. "But his contact list is pretty short. He doesn't have many friends he talks to on a regular basis."

"Well, there's one name I recognize," Aims said. "Looks like he stays in touch with White. Look at that. A couple of calls every day for the three days preceding the crash—and three on the day of the crash."

"The last one was a text message and must have been made just before the missile was fired," Rick observed. "Okay, he says, 'I've shot the two guys, have the briefcase, and am on my way out of the plane.'"

"Let's send the entire cell phone log to Brunswick. This is a smoking gun, but I think we're only seeing the tip of the iceberg.

"We need to know what Blackstone is up to with the Arabian prince. We could be looking at a disaster waiting to happen."

Chapter 7

The afternoon was spent cyber searching. Rick sent a request to Collier in the Brunswick office to have forensic accountants investigate both Blackstone's and the prince's family's investments and sources of income other than the royal family purse.

Aims was fortunate to find a recent article on the internet detailing the logistics of the prince's family travels. It detailed the entourage that accompanied them, with a group picture. Its publication was a radical departure from the usual cloak of secrecy that surrounded the family's doings, and the team put a lot of effort into blowing up the picture in order to have ID photos of the members of the group traveling with the prince and his sons on the *Obsidian*.

Following the evening meal, Aims and the team shared the results of the various aspects of their research. She learned that when the forensic accountants in Brunswick began to correlate their search of transactions between the Al Masih family and C. Arthur Blackstone, they found that the Al Masihs had already begun to invest in Blackstone's Onyx Group. Time had limited the amount of digging, but Aims was told that their home office thought that the team should have this much information before their upcoming interview with Blackstone. She agreed.

They discussed the watch schedule for the evening.

"I'm gonna move the *Chameleon* to a spot far enough away to make any nighttime visit from anybody a nightmare to plan and carry out," Orbison said. "But our daytime visit by the longboat's outboard will still work. No one should be able to figure out where the boat came from, an' that'll buy us some time if we need it. We still need ta keep watch."

Aims settled into her bunk, her brief evening prayers accompanied by the rhythmic throb of the *Chameleon*'s powerful engines moving them due west into the Gulf, away from the position from which their satellite communications had originated. While encrypted, there was an outside chance that the very act of communicating in code could have been detected. Better to be safe than sorry.

Lord, she prayed, *I'm working on this communication thing. So, although "Now I lay me down to sleep" is considered a child's prayer, this child needs Your protection. Your continued presence. Our whole team does. We've done all the research and preparation that we can. Now, I don't know any other thing to do but to put us and this whole undertaking in Your hands. Fulfill Your promise to us that only our eyes will observe the outcome of the wicked's behavior. And let us be able to detect what that wicked behavior is.*

In the meantime, give us rest and protection. Thank You.

It seemed she had just closed her eyes when Rick called her to stand her assigned watch. It would be first light soon. After standing her watch, she and Larry were chosen to be the ones to visit Blackstone and his guests on the *Obsidian*, to arrive around ten o'clock. It was an early start of what promised to be a long day. Seeing how little respect was accorded to the uniform of her fellow naval officers—how easy it was to kill them—she had no desire to wear *her* navy uniform for the visit. While not hiding her service rank, she would not make it a prominent part of her introduction of herself.

The *Chameleon* now lay northwest of Key West and due west of their target of *Obsidian*. Aims kept an eye on the monitors checking their approaches. Of particular concern to her was the sonar screen that was getting flickering images from time to time. Finally, when light was streaking the eastern horizon, an image began to take shape on the sonar. Aims was reaching for the radio to sound the alarm to Orbison and Rick when the water rippled and a pod of dolphins broached and began to leap in play around their boat. Pausing a moment to watch the beautiful, playful creatures, she jerked her attention back to the sonar. There had to be a reason for the dolphins to target the *Chameleon*. She reached for the call button while blessing Orbison's contacts in the Coast Guard. They had given him access to military-grade equipment that could distinguish between metallic and biologic objects. Were those humans on scooters?

When the men responded to her call, she spoke into her throat mic while hitting the button to raise the anchors and put the boat on the move. Turning sharply to starboard, she powered out into the Gulf, pushing to put as much distance between the dolphins and their human companions as fast as she could. She had them at three-quarters throttle when Orbison slid into his chair at the helm and took over for her.

"Did ya see what was in the water?" Orbison asked as he kept them accelerating.

"No, just got a register of a nonbiologic with two human biologic figures," she replied. "I figured we could check it out and identify exactly what is was when we had some distance from it." She was rewinding the monitor's recording as she spoke.

"Good thinking," Rick said as he joined her at the other station.

When Orbison had the *Chameleon* about ten nautical miles away from their earlier position, he began a sweeping turn and slowed them down to barely steerage. As they slowed, the monitors came back online as the speed of the water passing over the sensors came down. The sonar monitor was now clear of any images registering. Aims began to play the recording so they could check out the pod of dolphins and the metallic reading along with them.

Although the water was clear, the swimming sea mammals had roiled the bottom enough to cloud the images. And the metallic objects were moving slowly so as not to create a bow wave or wake. That coupled with the distance at which Aims had picked them up made it impossible to determine exactly what was there, but it was a pretty safe bet that there were a couple of humans swimming with the bottle-nosed dolphins, and they were using diver propulsion vehicles or underwater scooters.

While Rick and Aims were examining the recording, Orbison had gotten on the radio to the Coast Guard station at Fort Meyers Beach. He discovered that his friend Davy Jones was on duty.

"Why're you workin' today, Davy?" Orbison asked.

"Seems the secretary of the navy had some concerns over the deaths of a couple of his officers. He requested extra patrols to monitor civilian boat traffic around the Ten Thousand Islands Sanctuary."

"So, have you seen anything? Like this morning?"

"Just a boat coming out of the Everglades City marina. They had a diver in the water flag up, and when we asked what was going on, they said they had a couple of snowbirds who wanted to swim with the dolphins. Why?"

"We caught a blip on our sonar. What's the position of their dive boat?"

Davy read off the coordinates, and Orbison checked it on the chart. It was a probable source of what their sonar had registered.

"What'd the dive boat know about their snowbirds?"

"Just a couple of students from MIT taking a vacation with family friends in the Naples area. Daddy is some nabob from the Middle East. Is that a problem?"

"Could be. Dive boat operator didn't happen to give you their names by any chance?"

"Yeah, he did. But he couldn't pronounce 'em. He had to spell it out. Want 'em?"

"I do. Got a pencil and paper. Go."

When the Coastie finished reading off the names, he said to Orbison, "Does that help or even mean anything to you?"

"Yeah. Thanks, Davy. Lemme know when those two jokers come back up. Okay?"

Half an hour later, when Davy notified them that the dive boat had recovered their divers and were headed back to the Everglades City marina, Orbison had the *Chameleon* close to his chosen launch point for the longboat.

❧ ⁂ ☙

Aims and Larry were both wearing navy-issued casual clothing—khaki cargo pants with their badges and ID clipped to their belts.

The navy had recently upgraded all IDs with locator chips, similar to what some states were doing for driver's licenses and photo IDs. They wore zippered navy blue windbreakers over navy blue polo shirts. The shirts were new technology that incorporated a Kevlar-like material, providing some protection from bullets without the appearance of being body armor. In addition, they had the Naval Investigative Services logo embroidered in fine gold wire over the left pocket. Paired with the locator chip in their ID, they had a sender and receiver capability that allowed them to be located anywhere, even if surrounded by a signal-jamming field.

Although neither carried sidearms this time, both had backup weaponry. Larry had a throwing knife in its sheath behind his neck, and Aims had a stiletto in a sheath in her boot. Both weapons were ceramic, which were supposed to pass without a problem through any metal detector device. They hoped that without obvious firearms, they would eliminate any pat-down examination when they arrived.

Furthermore, when Aims's surgeons were putting her back together, some of her skeletal parts consisted of metal plates and screws. They told her that metal detectors were not recommended.

Aims and Larry were ready to board the longboat to head for *Obsidian* and a visit with C. Arthur Blackstone and possibly his guests. They had been running the search on the two divers whose names Davy had provided. Their connection to the Blackstones quickly became apparent.

Just before Aims stepped on board the longboat, she sought out Rick.

"Rick," she said. "I need a favor."

"Sure, Aims. Anything."

"I need you to pray with me for our safety. I feel like Daniel entering the lion's den."

"You are," Rick said, taking both her hands as they bowed their heads close together.

"Lord," he prayed, "Aims and Larry are headed for the lion's den. Like Daniel, please guard them as You guarded Your prophet. We thank You and praise You."

"Thanks, Rick. I needed that."

Larry boarded the outboard first and took his place at the throttles. As Aims joined him, Orbison touched her shoulder and murmured, "Watch yourselves, Commander."

"Will do, Chief," she replied. "Keep your eye on us." She seated herself behind Larry and said, "Okay, Larry. Let's get this show on the road." The boat did a sweeping turn to port and headed for the coordinates that their research showed was the location of Blackstone's yacht.

Larry guided the outboard to the transom of the *Obsidian*. Their research told them this was the yacht's boathouse entrance. There was an intercom console mounted to the hull with a small video camera on display. Aims pressed the button, holding her credentials in view of the camera. When a voice responded, requesting what was wanted, Aims said, "Navy investigators, Larry Robb and Amelia Wallace, to talk to Mr. Blackstone about the crash of his jet a few days ago. Permission to come aboard?"

"Wait one," came the reply.

After a few moments, the door to the boathouse area on their left began to rise. "Please enter the boathouse," the voice said, "and tie your craft. Someone will meet you and take you to Mr. Blackstone. Welcome aboard."

Larry and Aims had just secured the line of the longboat when a crewman came in the boathouse area from somewhere within the *Obsidian.* He stepped forward and offered Aims a hand as she prepared to disembark. Larry joined her unassisted.

"This way please," he said, gesturing to the automated glass doors leading into the yacht's interior.

As Aims looked at the doorframe of the glass doors, she noted the sensor eyes embedded within it.

"Excuse me please," she said, laying a hand on the crewman's arm. "Does passage through that doorway mean we're passing through a metal detector?"

"Yes, ma'am, it does. The insurance company requires standard TSA safety measures to prevent being boarded by pirates. Visitors have to immediately pass through this doorway whenever we're at sea. Will that be a problem?"

"Well, I'm afraid so." Aims smiled. "You see, when I crashed my fighter on the deck of an aircraft carrier in the Persian Gulf, they patched me together with metal pins and plates. They said passage through metal detectors would not be recommended for the rest of my life and that I should warn operators of those devices about my aversion to them. If such a procedure is required, perhaps you have a wand or something to replace it. Sorry to be a problem."

"Not a problem, ma'am," he replied. "We'll use the wand on both of you. Some of Mr. Blackstone's guests have pacemakers, and we're prepared for that." He smiled graciously at them both, deactivated the sensors in the doorjamb, and swept them both with the wand before ushering them into the yacht's interior.

They were taken through a maze of corridors and up an elevator that opened into the entrance of an opulent salon. Colorful Persian carpets softened their footsteps, and tapestry-like drapes were pulled back to afford a 180-degree panorama of sea views. Their host and hostess rose from a plush sofa fronted by a glass-topped cocktail table that held a coffee pot being kept warm over a small flame, as well as decorated cups with no handles.

C. Arthur Blackstone was a tall man, over six feet tall, with a trim but not buff figure. He wore a crisp, cotton, button-down dress shirt with long sleeves precisely rolled to just below the elbow. The medium blue stripes on a white background complemented the navy gabardine dress slacks that were sharply creased and stacked fashionably over his tan penny loafers. His full head of hair was just beginning to show some gray threads, but his blue eyes displayed an intense interest in his surroundings. His open, easy smile seemed to be habitual, if the laugh lines around his eyes and brackets at the corners of his mouth were to be believed.

Beside him was a trim, attractive woman. Her head would probably reach his chin, and her figure was obviously the result of an intense program of athletic activities and a consistent exercise regimen. She sported an attractive Florida tan. At first glance, she could have been mistaken for a vapid, almost trophy wife whose total concern was her appearance. But Aims had some experience with high-society wives, including her own mother, and she had learned to look deeper for signs of intelligence and wit hiding behind the social camouflage.

"Welcome to the *Obsidian*," Mr. Blackstone said, extending his hand to greet them. "I'm Art Blackstone. This is my wife, Alexa. Would you care to join us? We're just having morning coffee." He motioned to the sofa, but Aims chose the matching side chair to his left, and Larry moved to the one to the right of the sofa. Only then did the investigators reach out to shake the Blackstones' hands. Their show of independence with their choice of seating sparked a barely noticeable narrowing of Blackstone's eyes, but Aims saw it as her hand grasped his. When she gripped Alexa's hand, Aims saw the twinkle of recognition in the other woman's eyes. Before Aims could introduce herself, Blackstone continued speaking.

"Commander Wallace, so good to see you. White described you and expressed concern that you had not called to get our coordinates here. I told him not to worry. I said that any investigator worth his or her salt should be able to locate that information without our help. I see that I was right."

"Thank you, Mr. Blackstone. It is nice to meet you."

"Please call me Art," he replied. "Do they call you Amelia?"

"No, sir. I answer to Aims," she said. "It was my call sign when I flew fighters in the Persian Gulf, and it stuck."

"Oh my," said Alexa. "I'm impressed."

Blackstone turned to Larry. "White said that the lovely commander was accompanied by a couple of gentlemen, but he did not have your names."

"I'm Special Agent Larry Robb," he replied, accepting the offered hand. He noted the firm, slight challenge of Blackstone's grip without responding to it.

"Welcome, Agent. Please be seated. How about that coffee? We are offering you authentic Arabian coffee. It's a gift from our house guests from the Kingdom of Arabia." He waved his hand to the exotic coffee service before them as he seated himself. Alexa, with perfect southern manners, busied herself pouring.

"It is a traditional Arabian blend, served boiling hot, so please be careful. My guest tells me that it is served in his country as a ceremonial gesture of kindness and hospitality. It is in that spirit that we offer it to you. It is traditionally served with dates. Alexa has had his waiter teach her the nuances of the ceremony. She will serve you a small amount, because it is so hot, but will offer you as many refills as you wish. Please enjoy."

When the ceremonial service of their refreshment was complete, the Blackstones leaned back on the sofa and regarded their visitors.

"This is lovely," Aims began. "Thank you both for the beautiful ceremonial welcome.

"We do need to ask you some questions about the crash of your plane and the deaths of its occupants. Sorry to inject a bit of unpleasantness into this serene setting. We hope you have no objection to a recording of our conversation. I assure you, it is protocol."

"We understand, Aims," Blackstone replied. Aims tagged the beginning of the recording with identifying information and then nodded to Blackstone. "White mentioned that your team was taking the lead initially here in Florida," he said, "and that the NTSB would be joining you all in Georgia. I'm sure that you'll need to dot the i's and cross the t's for them. I'm assuming this interview and all of your investigation here is just a formality, conducted on behalf of a sister agency."

"Well," Aims replied with a smile, "not exactly." Before they embarked on this expedition, the team had agreed to avoid discussing the gunshot wounds and the missile with Blackstone. After all, they were not sure of his role, if any, in the whole episode. They needed to gauge his level of involvement.

"I'd be surprised if you find evidence of pilot error," Blackstone said. "Joe Grimes was an excellent pilot and meticulous in his inspection and maintenance of the equipment. Was there enough left in the wreckage to find the flight recorders? White said he saw parts of the plane flying in all directions. He thought there was probably very little left to tell you what happened."

"The plane did not really disintegrate," Larry said. "We actually located and loaded a few pretty big pieces to take back to our office in Georgia for analysis."

"Does that mean that you did locate flight recorders?" Alexa asked.

"We did not actually hold them in our hands," Aims said. "But according to the specs of that model of Cessna, the parts of the fuselage where the recorders would be located were intact. FAA regulations require that the location of these instruments be pretty rugged, capable of withstanding a lot of punishment. I'm sure that feature of your plane was mentioned at the time you made your purchase."

"Since we didn't find pilot error or equipment failure," Larry inserted, "we have to wonder what could have caused your plane to go down. Didn't White say he saw a fireball, Aims?"

"Yes, Larry, he did. Which brings up another question. We have no doubt that your assessment of your pilot is accurate. After all, Art, who knows your employees better than you? So, if there was no pilot error or equipment failure, then what are we left with? The conclusion that the crash was not an unfortunate accident?"

"Wait a minute," Alexa said. "What exactly are you saying?" Her husband's eyes, narrowed slightly, were fixed on Aims's face, and the length of his right index finger moved rhythmically across the line of his tightly clamped lips.

"Art, Alexa," Aims said, "we're just asking questions. I mean, think about it. This is your plane, flown by your employee, carrying your guests to visit you on your lovely yacht. It seems only logical that we would want to know what you think is going on."

After a long moment of silence and a deep sigh, Blackstone spoke. "Tell me again why your team is conducting this investigation and not the NTSB."

"We think that should be obvious," Larry said. "We found a three-star admiral assigned to the Pentagon and his aide among the victims of the crash of your plane. The navy takes jurisdiction in investigating the deaths of its officers."

"It has just occurred to me," Aims said. "Art, could *you* or Alexa be the ultimate target of this horrible act?"

"What exactly do you mean, Aims?"

"I just went through it," she said. "Your plane, your pilot, your guests coming to visit you. I think it would be a mistake to rush to judgment until we find out what you may know or think about this. There is a possibility that you know more than you are aware of. Since you were notified of the crash, have you had any thoughts that might give us a lead?"

"I can't think what you could mean."

"Okay, Art," she said. "First of all, whose idea was Admiral Carter's visit to you? Was he in the habit of coming to see you for a few days of fishing? Were you, Alexa, and he close friends?"

Blackstone gazed sharply at both Aims and Larry before allowing his eyes to turn toward his wife, and then stray to the beautiful seascape beyond the high glass walls.

"You know," he said, "now that you mention it, we *were* surprised when he contacted us and asked if he could spend a day or so fishing the Gulf. He'd only been here once, right after the Onyx Group was awarded the last contract for targeting chips. We had a nice visit then, but I wouldn't say we became close friends. Would you, Alexa?" When she shook her head, he continued. "So, for him to invite himself for a few days of fishing, it was a little unusual. More than a little unusual, now that I think about it. A lot unusual."

"We always try to stress to our guests that they are welcome to come and spend some time on the water," Alexa said. "Whenever the mood strikes. So we didn't really give it a lot of thought at the time."

"But looking back now," Blackstone said, "I realize that I just dismissed it as someone taking us at our word—without taking into account the admiral's characteristic reserve in his dealings with me throughout the process of getting the details of the defense contract ironed out. Now I see that his request was very much out of character for him. It should have raised some red flags, but it didn't. I'm sorry about that now. In hindsight, we should have paid more attention."

"You said he had only been here once before," Larry said. "What was the date of that visit?"

"It was when we signed the final contract between Onyx and the Department of Defense. I remember he said something like, 'I'm not a mother hen type. I don't look over the shoulder of my contractors. You won't hear from me unless there is something I need to discuss with you.'"

"How long ago was that?" Aims asked.

"Oh, let me think. About seven or eight months, wasn't it, Alexa?"

"That sounds right," she replied.

"Did you have any communication with him during that time?"

"No. I figured no communication meant that things were going okay."

"A reasonable conclusion," Larry said, "in light of his statement about not looking over your shoulder."

"Let me ask another question," Aims said. "We are discussing the assumption that Admiral Carter was a secondary target but that you, Art, could be the primary target. Let's say, for the sake of argument, that you in some way might have been the indirect target of your plane's crash. Who would want to take such a shot at you?

"And if they wanted to take a shot at you, why not make it a direct shot? Why go through a three-star admiral on the Pentagon staff? Seems like that's knocking down a hornet's nest to get someone stung. Lots of element of chance."

"Or maybe it was two birds, one stone," Larry said quietly.

"How would that work?" Alexa asked.

"Let's follow the line of Admiral Carter's policy of no communication unless there is a problem," Aims said. "If Carter invited himself to a fishing trip with you, maybe you should consider that there has been a problem he wanted to discuss with you face-to-face. If that was the case, then preventing such a face-to-face discussion might seem desirable. So, now we're back to my question. Who would take such a shot at you and the admiral?"

"Wow, guys," Alexa said. "That question takes the sun right out of my sky. Do you think Admiral Carter was coming to discuss a problem?"

"Well," Aims said, "possibly. I have another question. Why didn't you return to Marco Island to see what was going on after the plane crashed?"

"I mentioned returning to my estate manager, White," Blackstone said. "I asked him if you were going to need me there, and he said that the plane had totally disintegrated and that there wasn't enough left to provide many clues. He said that the investigators would be able to get anything needed from a simple phone call. That my other guests would not be happy to have their trip cut short. So we stayed out here. I can see now how that could have been a huge error, from several perspectives."

"I'm getting the vibe that White's assessment was inaccurate, to say the least," Alexa said.

"To say the least," Aims agreed. "I take it that such an inaccuracy is not common for White. That his usual opinions have been accurate enough to cause you to trust what he advises."

"That would be the case. White and I have been working together most of our lives."

"Tell me about White, Art," Aims said.

Blackstone and Alexa looked at each other for a long moment. Alexa reach over to take her husband's hand.

"Let me think," Blackstone said. "He and I have known each other forever. I think we first met in kindergarten, if you can imagine that. His family lived just down the block from my mom and me in West Miami. We became friends on our first day of school and have been close friends ever since.

"We watched our neighborhood change with the influx of Cuban and Central American immigrants. Our neighborhood became a barrio ruled by Latino gangs by the time we were in high school. White and I faced a lot of peer pressure to join one of the gangs in our hood.

"My mom, being a single parent, spent a lot of time and energy to keep me in school, keep my grades up, and work hard for a better life. Over the years of grade school, White spent a lot of time in our home. Both his parents worked, so there wasn't much supervision for him there. Mom made it fun for him to be with us, but she also made it clear that there were rules, and he was expected to abide by them, just like I was. If he slipped up, she'd call him on it. He always took whatever criticism or punishment she dished out."

"I've always been sorry that I never got to know my mother-in-law," Alexa said. "By the time Art and I met in college, she had passed on. But I've always been impressed by Art's stories about her, as well as by the good man she raised Art to be." The two exchanged smiles.

"Thanks to her," Blackstone continued, "both White and I won academic scholarships to the University of Florida at Gainesville. We worked the docks at the Port of Miami on our school vacations. We had to work hard, but both of us learned the benefit of hard work and following the rules. So, after all these years, why wouldn't I trust him now?"

"We understand that. When you put it that way, we can see your point," Larry said.

"So, getting back to our question," Aims said. "If Admiral Carter was coming to discuss a problem with you, who would want to prevent that?"

"And I'm asking again," Blackstone said. "Do you have any reason to think that was the purpose of his trip? I'll accept that inviting himself for a vacation does seem out of character for Admiral Carter. But do we have a reason to believe that coming here was for any other purpose than rest and recreation?"

"As I mentioned before," Aims said, "possibly. Larry told you that the navy takes jurisdiction when there are deaths of any naval or Marine Corps personnel."

"How do you know that those on board the plane did not

parachute out before it crashed? If the plane disintegrated, they could have escaped. Have you had the Coast Guard involved in search and rescue?" Alexa asked.

"Well, first of all," Aims said, "the plane did not disintegrate. In fact, as we said earlier, we found quite large pieces of wreckage. And bodies. We think that one of them was Admiral Carter. So again, who do you think would want to prevent him from meeting with you?"

"I don't know," Blackstone replied. His scowl was intense. "I'll have to think about that. Why wouldn't Admiral Carter communicate with me by email or letter? I got the feeling that a face-to-face with a contractor would be a measure of last resort."

"Well," Larry said, "that is why we are asking these questions. Do we know for certain that there were no prior communications before he asked to meet with you?"

"Are you suggesting that he sent messages that Art did not get?" Alexa asked.

When the two investigators kept silent, watching his face, Blackstone spoke. "Now I'll have to do some investigating at Onyx Group headquarters to find out the answer to that myself."

"Well," Aims said, "as an assist to you in that process, we have a tidbit for you. Our boss, the secretary of the navy, did some checking with Admiral Carter's office. Admiral Carter was sort of a workaholic. Whenever he went anywhere, he always took work along with him. If that work involved sensitive papers, he made copies of them and left a list of what he had with him so there would be no possible breach of national security. A check of that list indicated some of the communications were with Onyx about the targeting chips your company is providing. I'm telling you this because it might be a place to start looking." Aims stood, and Larry followed suit. "It has been a pleasure to meet both of you," she said, offering her hand.

The Blackstones stood as well. "Aims, we really appreciate your visit. I want you to know that I am pretty concerned about all of this. I didn't know how serious the situation was, with the Pentagon and all, and I assure you that we will get to the bottom of this. I'll be looking at my entire organization to see exactly what is going on.

"I came up the hard way, but I consider myself a patriot. I've been proud to be able to provide assistance to our military operations, and if someone is messing with my company and its product, I intend to put a stop to it."

"Good," Aims replied. She handed him her business card. "This will give you contact information at our office in Brunswick. Just be smart and stay safe. Remember that navy officers in uniform have died and that is a serious thing, so watch your step. We hope to be back in Georgia soon, so if you come up with anything, please give us a call there."

"Thank you. I will. Come on. We'll walk you down to your boat. If I need to speak with you while you're still here, can your office in Georgia make that happen?"

"Yes, they can," Larry interjected.

The four of them descended through the corridors and elevator of the *Obsidian*, exchanging innocuous comments about the beauty of Blackstone's yacht and the day outside. They shook hands again, and Aims and Larry embarked on the outboard, then exited through the boathouse door and out into the Gulf.

Chapter 8

Larry guided the boat in a long, sweeping curve toward the southwest after they cleared the opening in the boathouse of the *Obsidian*. As they cleared the apex of the curve, Aims activated their comm link with the *Chameleon* and called Orbison and Rick.

"Hey, Aims," Rick responded. "We're locked onto your signal."

"Good," she said. "That's what I wanted you to do. Can you observe any underwater activity around us? I don't want us to pick up a tail coming at you."

"We are doing routine stuff. But if you're feeling a little threatened, we can step it up to the next level."

"Please do that. I'm worried about scuba divers on scooters picking us up as we clear the yacht."

"Okay. The chief is doing that now. What happened at that interview that you are coming away so jittery?"

"I don't want to give details over the air. You can listen to the recording when we get there. Suffice it to say that things are murkier, not clearer. We're walking through the lions' hunting ground carrying a fresh kill, so to speak."

"Gotcha. Tell Larry to activate his GPS navigation feature of the longboat's helm. It's programmed to respond only to the *Chameleon*'s signal. It will chart a safe course and bring you straight on in. Chief says you're about thirty minutes out at three-quarter throttle."

Their actual rendezvous took longer because Orbison detected activity, both surface and underwater, along their back trail. Rick called Aims and Larry about it.

"Chief says to open that throttle all the way. We are seeing signs of snoopers on your back trail. Your join-up is going to be a running catch with both of us on the move. He wanted to know if that would be a problem, and I assured him that it was a procedure that we practiced in Brunswick from time to time. So don't mess it up and make me look bad."

"Not a problem, boss," Larry said into the speakers. "Thanks for the heads-up. We won't do any damage to your reputation or ours."

When they were safely on board at the dive station, Aims spoke to Rick.

"Before we stow this thing, we need to do a close examination of the underside. I checked as closely as I could while we were on approach, but this baby sat unattended for a while, unprotected and in what might be considered enemy territory. If we picked up activity on our back trail, there could be a tracker attached out of sight from above the water line."

"Chief already thought of that, Aims," Rick said as he and Larry upended the boat and began examination.

Just then, Rick's phone buzzed. "Yeah, Chief? ... Okay, I'll tell them."

He broke the connection and then said, "Chief says hang on. We're making a top-speed getaway from this position."

The search was a little difficult, given that the three of them always had to have one hand gripping a hand rail, but finally they found a small, state-of-the-art RFID chip secured behind the outboard motor of the boat. They crushed it underfoot before throwing it into the wake of the *Chameleon* while speeding into the open water of the Gulf of Mexico. Then the team joined Orbison topside.

"Hi, y'all," he said. "I could just about peg when that bug quit sendin' info. All of a sudden, they literally began goin' in circles, trying to find where you'd gone. Good job. I picked a spot opposite Highland Pointe off the coast below Naples. It'll give us with some breathin' room while we regroup and decide what we're gonna do next."

"Great, Chief," Rick said. "I want to listen to the recording of the Blackstones' interview, and then we'll check in with Collier and let him know what's going on."

By the time they had finished, Orbison had the *Chameleon* sloop-rigged and was navigating past Highland Pointe into the maze of waterways threaded through the Big Cypress National Preserve. Larry now occupied the fighting chair whose fishing pole holder was wired to send and receive on the military encrypted satellite. Rick and Aims were composing the message that would be sent via a burst to their office in Georgia.

Teleconferences and chats were risky because the very process of broadcasting could give away their position. But notification of the results of their interview with Blackstone was necessary. So the burst was the best compromise. During the run-in from their position far out in the Gulf, the team and Orbison discussed the interview with Blackstone and his wife and bandied it back and forth, whether he was trying to snow them or whether he really was unaware of the targeting chips' malfunction and Admiral Carter's dissatisfaction with Onyx Group's lack of response to their inquiries.

"I find myself wondering at his allusion to White while he was speaking about his pride of country. Who was he trying to convince, himself or you?" Rick said.

"It didn't raise any flags at the time, but now that you mention it, maybe it should have," Larry responded.

"What about you, Aims?"

"You know …" Aims's demeanor was thoughtful. "I could picture those two as teenagers trying to buck the gangs of their hood. I could see Blackstone coming right out in open opposition, but I could see White trying to skate the line between the two cultures. That seems to come closest to my impressions from talking with both men. I don't know how to characterize it better than I see Blackstone as a doer and White as a climber. Or maybe Blackstone is the brawn of the pair, and White thinks he's the brains. White would have few qualms about the thickness of the ice if he wanted to get somewhere or do something. Nor would he have any scruples about keeping Blackstone unaware of any of his wheeling and dealing, even when he made promises about what Blackstone would or would not do. I think he would make a promise to one group and then manipulate the other side into going along. What about that assessment, Chief? Does that match with your impressions?"

Orbison stared thoughtfully into space for a long moment before he brought his gaze back to Aims.

"You know, Commander," he said, "I've been paintin' both Blackstone and White with the same dirty brush. But I gotta confess that I realize now that I've not spent near the same amount of time with Art Blackstone as with White."

"What was the occasion or occasions of your interaction with White?" Rick had been staring intently at the former navy chief petty officer.

"Well," Orbison began, "when Blackstone first bought his estate on Marco Island, Collier County required an inspection by the county fire department. That inspection was assigned to our station, 'cause we're closest. When he bought his island, which he named Obsidian Haven, the Coast Guard had me accompany their inspection as the local government representative. Both times, White was the owner's agent that we dealt with.

"Come to think about it, we did not interact with Blackstone at all. Either of those times. So, I guess my attitude toward Blackstone is actually unfair. Not based on any interaction with the man. That being said, Rick," he went on, "I gotta admit that I think the commander is spot-on." He turned again to Aims. "I guess I should've taken the time ta deal directly with Blackstone before lettin' my opinion of him harden like I did. Makes me wonder how much wheelin' and dealin' White has done in his boss's name. I'd say it's a good bet that your interview has been a wake-up call. I wouldn't be surprised if White goes through a performance review like nothin' he's ever had from Blackstone. I just hope that Blackstone is smart enough to keep his diggin' to himself until he knows just how much danger he could be in."

"I think you're right, Chief," Aims said. "I also think that what he finds could have an impact on a lot of people—us, his family, and national security in general."

❦ ❧

After their detailed report to Brunswick of the interview with Blackstone, the team each took an assigned task. Larry returned to the fighting chair with the antenna fishing rod in place. He had a tablet in his hands, connected to the *Chameleon*'s encrypted system to receive incoming communication bursts from the home office. Orbison was concentrating on navigating the meandering coastal waterway, working their way back toward the Gulf. Rick was in the bridge house with him, keeping close watch on the monitor screens that were so crucial to their safety. Aims was in the galley. With so many tasks to keep up with and varied watch schedules, meals had become an individual enterprise. She had made a turkey, lettuce, and tomato sandwich, paired with a steaming mug of herbal tea. Her day began early, and it was now well into the afternoon. The thought of some rack time was pulling at her, and she hoped the light meal would be just enough to allow for some sleep. Her next scheduled watch at the monitors was only a few hours away.

She was washing down the last bite when the message alert chimed on the plasma screen in the salon. She rose and was headed that way when Larry burst into the salon, waving his tablet. Rick was on his heels. With a few keystrokes, Larry opened the encrypted message on the plasma screen. It was a text message from their boss.

"Relaying this message for Commander Wallace from Art Blackstone. 'Sorry I can't keep our next appointment. Just opened a new can of Arabian coffee—full of worms. Fishing spoiled due to presence of great white. Trying not to become POW. Contact you later. Art on the run.' Does that mean what it looks like?"

"Wow," Larry said. "For an amateur civilian, that's a pretty nifty code."

Rick turned to him. "What does it mean to you?"

"Blackstone told us that the Arabian coffee he served us was a gift from his guests. We know that means Abbud Al Masih and his two sons. We know what 'full of worms' means."

"Okay," Rick said. "Good. Looks like he is seeing his lifelong buddy, White, to be a cruising shark looking for blood in the water. Agree with that, Aims?"

"Agreed," she said. "I think the POW remark means trying not to get caught, and being on the run means that he's going to be out of touch for a while. Looks like he touched a nerve."

"Larry," said Rick, "text Collier back with what we just said. Sounds like a good job of decoding, team."

While Larry worked on their reply, Aims looked over at Rick. "Could we find out what is in the Arabian coffee can of worms?"

"Possibly," Rick said. "Any contracts and agreements made by American corporations are supposed to be public record. I wonder if our forensic accountants have found anything yet."

"Larry," Aims said. "Can you add that question to your text?"

"Sure thing, Skipper. You caught it just in time."

"Guys," Aims said, stifling a huge yawn, "I'm on overtime. I need to get some rest before my next watch. If you need me ... please don't call me unless we're being boarded by hostiles."

"Okay, Aims." Rick chuckled. "Hopefully it won't come to that. Sleep tight."

By the time Aims reached her cabin, fatigue was pulling at her like undertow. She closed the door behind her, the sight of the taut bedspread beckoning. Then she caught sight of the wooden valet bolted to the bulkhead beside the door. Her training sessions for the Ready Five Alert Squadron on the carrier played back for her, and she knew there were some things that *had* to be done before she could surrender to sleep. It was okay, even preferable, that she sleep in her clothes. But her boots needed to be placed, toes in, in front of the valet, and her windbreaker hung over its arms. Next, she checked the slide action and magazine load of her weapon, before chambering a round with the safety switch on and placing the weapon and her credentials on the seat of the valet. If she was called before her scheduled watch, she would be armed and ready for whatever might await her on the other side of the door. Now, she could give in and stretch across the waiting mattress. Her last conscious thought was *Sleeping, Lord. Watch over …*

It must have been the joking reference to being boarded that prompted Aims's mind to create a scenario where she was in a smoke-filled passage, trying to follow Rick into the salon. She struggled to see him ahead of her. Suddenly she realized that Rick was pounding on her door.

"Aims, Aims. Wake up, Aims. Boarders. Come on. We need you."

The next thing she knew, she was standing by the door, booted with her stiletto still in place, jacketed with credentials in her pocket, her weapon in her hand, pointed skyward.

She opened her door, and Rick motioned her to follow as he turned toward the salon. There was smoke everywhere, but it looked like it was from a smoke grenade and not a fire. Topside, she heard men shouting, the rhythmic three-shot stutter of the deck-mounted Browning machine gun in the hands of Chief Orbison, punctuated by the staccato boom of Larry Robb on a rifle. She knew it was Larry because he was the office deadeye with a rifle or shotgun, while she was the reigning queen of the target pistols. She hoped those two hillbilly hunters were having a good night.

A wave of Rick's hand sent her toward the port passage leading to the foredeck as he went starboard. She had just entered the short passage when she saw the foot of a dark-clad figure, toes down and obviously slithering backward on its stomach to enter the passage from the deck. Flicking off the safety, she placed the red dot of her laser target on the heel and squeezed the trigger. The foot jerked at the impact of the nine-millimeter shot and rotated as the figure came upright. She recognized the distinctive outline of the Uzi he held. Without hesitation, she placed the red target dot on the weapon and fired again. The intruder emitted another shout of pain before someone grabbed the back of his shirt collar and pulled him backward toward the prow of the yacht.

Then Aims realized that the shots and shouts topside had diminished, so she took a chance and charged out onto the deck. The intruders' longboat was disappearing into their self-generated smoke screen, and the others were gathered around Orbison at the gun mount.

When she walked up, Rick was speaking.

"Okay, Chief, where are we?"

"Not too bad. I alerted the Coast Guard about this. I requested the SAR crew ta be on the lookout for that longboat."

"How did they get on board, Chief?" she asked.

"A diversion," Larry said. "Proximity fuse torpedo that did not do as much damage as they thought it would. Probably the shallow water here."

"Not only that," Orbison said. "It hit the housing of the retractable counter board. It's a strong piece of armor. My buddy Jones is sendin' a tow boat to take the *Chameleon* back to the station at Fort Meyers Beach. So we'll check 'er over an' repair 'er."

Rick and Aims looked at each other for a long moment.

Afterward, each nodded, and Rick said, "Chief, we need to get back to Brunswick. I don't think there is much more information we can dig up out here without getting someone killed. Whatever we need to do, we can do from Brunswick. What about an SAR chopper to take us to the Marco Island Airport?"

"I agree with that," Orbison said. "Whatever gear is still on board here, or the *Maisie Mae,* or the *Lindy Lou*, I'll ship to you. I'll also get my girl, Maisie, to return your rental car for you."

"That would be great, Chief," Aims said. "Add all those costs to your invoice. And the cost of whatever repairs you need here."

"Don't worry about that, Commander," he said with an awkward pat on her shoulder. "I may not be on active duty any longer, but I'm still in the service of my country. I'll call up that chopper for you." He turned and ascended to the bridge house.

Chapter 9

At the Marco Island Airport, the Coast Guard SAR pilot left the rotors slowly turning as the three investigators jumped down from the chopper to the tarmac, where their own chopper awaited them. As soon as his passengers were clear, the search and rescue pilot powered up and was gone. There were only a couple of choppers parked there, so it was not hard for them to recognize the one they wanted. With her duffel slung over one shoulder, Aims headed toward the pilot's door on the right, while Rick and Larry slung their duffel bags into the chopper before heading for the tie-downs.

Her hand had just released the latch on the door when she realized what had been bothering her from the moment her feet touched the pavement. All of the gauges were lit and registering. As that awareness spiked through her, the rotors over her head began to turn, and she felt movement behind her. She started to turn, thinking it was Rick behind her. She felt a sharp, painful blow to the back of her head, and her vision narrowed like a camera lens closing. She thought she heard a shout before the darkness enfolded her.

Someone was playing "The Anvil Chorus," and Aims's head was the drum set. The metronome was set at the speed of her heart rate. Awareness was slow in arriving, but finally her brain began to pose questions. *Where am I? Don't know. Can't see. Don't hear anything. Wait a minute. Yes, I do. Sounds like seagulls outside. Palm branches clacking together. Outside of what? Don't know. Can't see. Why can't I see? Can I see my hand? Can't move my hand. Why not? Behind my back. Tied. Not metal, so not handcuffs. My feet? Tied together. Lying down. On what? Not a bed. Not the bare floor either. It's so dark. Are my eyes open? Can't blink. Why? Could be a blindfold. I'll call for help. Can't open my mouth. Taped shut. Don't tell me. Duct tape. Well, that's original. Oh, God. They're using sensory deprivation.*

Aims spent some time forcing herself to breathe through the mind's panic response. Now she understood why Rick and her folks were so insistent that prayer helped. *Okay, Lord. You have my attention. All of it. I don't have any choice here. So, now is a good time for You to step in and display Your grace and power. I know that I don't deserve Your help, but I need it. And when this is over, I'll be sure to give You all the credit for Your deliverance, regardless of what method You use to accomplish it. I've been told that You know our hearts and thoughts, so You know how grateful I am to be alive. And how grateful I will be for Your strength to deal with whatever bad stuff is coming. I'm sure there will be bad stuff, and a lot of it, and I know myself not to be able to do this by my own strength.* Calm washed through her. Not knowing what else to do, she decided to rest, and she must have slept.

She awoke to an engulfing, burning pain as the tape was ripped away from her eyes and mouth. She screamed, trying to breathe again. She struggled to focus her eyes, after having had them forcibly closed for so long. As her vision cleared, she saw that two men were standing over her.

"Hello, Commander Wallace." She had heard that voice before but could not immediately put a name to it. "I admire your intestinal fortitude, being able to sleep at a time like this."

The cruel, rapid removal of the dense adhesive from the most sensitive areas of her face had caused a swamping sensory overload. The answering rush of adrenaline was a soothing touch. Then her thought processes seemed to come back online.

First came the memory of her surrendering prayer and the realization that she was now experiencing the answer to it. Next came the almost palpable cooling of the burning pain. Then she realized that her vision was returning to normal, as well as her recollection about the voice. The calm sound of her own voice surprised her.

"Hello, White. What are we doing here? Wherever here is."

"We are here, Commander," he said, "because I need to know what you have done with Mr. Blackstone."

"I have done nothing with Mr. Blackstone," she said. "The last time I saw him, he was waving goodbye to Larry and me as we left the boathouse enclosure on board the *Obsidian*. I can't tell you exactly how long ago that was, because I do not know how much time has elapsed since I started to board our helicopter to return to base in Georgia.

"I gotta tell you, though, this is the most rudely done questioning anyone has subjected me to—ever."

Her remark was greeted with a sharp, painful blow to the jaw. It was delivered by the dark-skinned, bearded man standing next to White and was accompanied by some words in a foreign language that did not sound polite. In the long silence that ensued, there were several more such painful blows—so many, in fact, that Aims lost count of them.

"Now, Commander," White said, "I'll ask you again. What have you done with Mr. Blackstone?"

"Are you saying that you don't know where Mr. Blackstone is?"

Another sharp, painful blow.

"I'll take that as a yes," Aims said, breathing heavily. Again, the response was a sharp, painful blow.

"Come on, White," Aims said when she could breathe over the pain that was nearly smothering her. "This is an extreme response to not being able to find your boss. And the potential loss of a valuable defense contract, don't you think? You're a smarter man than this. This course of behavior cannot end well for either you or your boss. Whether you believe me or not, I have no idea where your boss is. More slaps on the face will not change that."

"Don't patronize me, Commander," White growled. "I know that his last phone call was a text message to you. Where did he tell you he would meet you next time?"

"If you know that his last call was a text message, then you should be able to retrieve the message itself."

"We did. Where was his next appointment with you to take place?"

"We didn't decide on one. Have your pet gorilla hit me again if you want. But that's the truth."

Now it was White's companion who was growling, drawing back his hand for another hard slap. White's hand on his arm halted its motion.

"The navy has this all wrong, Commander," White said. His

upper lip was curled in derision. "The targeting chip that the admiral was monitoring was not the bread and butter product of Onyx Group. It's really small potatoes. The production of chips is not going to be affected one way or another by Blackstone's whereabouts."

"Then what is this all about?"

"Maybe I'll tell you. You're not going to live long enough to relay the information to anyone anyway. Onyx Group is working on a deal that will make Arabian oil production a sideline. It came from one of Art Blackstone's ideas while we were in college. He needs to be here to finish this project. We're ready to finalize this, and he needs to sign off on his part of the deal.

"So, you see, Commander, your little penny-ante investigation of a plane crash is just a speed bump. I'm giving you one last chance to save yourself from further suffering."

"White," she said. "I cannot tell you what I don't know. I really don't know where he is. I had no idea he was going anywhere."

❦ ❧

Rick and Larry were just reaching for the tie-downs of their helicopter when the engine powered up and the rotors began spinning over their heads. Rick threw himself onto the ground to avoid being struck by the chopper's undercarriage as it lifted away from them. The realization that Aims had been taken nearly kept Rick on his knees. He felt a rising cry in his chest. *No! Don't touch her. Bring her back.* He caught sight of Larry, out of the corner of his eye, coming to his feet. *Still have a job to do. A team.* While he wordlessly committed Aims to the Holy Spirit's care, he began to think of what he could do to get Aims back.

"You okay, Larry?" he called, coming upright.

"Good, boss. What is the Skipper doing?"

"She didn't do that," Rick said. "She didn't have time to even get into the chopper, let alone power up and take off. Now that I think about it, the turbine was already turning as we approached."

"So her departure was involuntary. Guess we better let somebody know," Larry said.

"Yeah, right," Rick said. "Why don't you let Orbison and the Coast Guard know? I'll alert Collier and get them tuning into her tracker frequency. No telling what kind of grief she is facing."

Both of them finished with their cell phones about the same time.

"Okay," Larry said, slipping the phone into the pocket of his windbreaker. "Orbison and his buddy in search and rescue are on their way here. Be here inside of ten minutes."

"Good," Rick said. "Collier says that SECNAV has authorized the release of Aims's tracker frequency to the Coast Guard station search and rescue chopper from the encrypted military satellite right away. So, now we wait for our taxi. Let's see what weaponry we have on us. We'll want to be locked and loaded when they get here for us. We gotta get these guys."

Rick and Larry spent the few minutes checking that their sidearms were ready and that they had spare magazines within easy reach. While he worked, Rick was praying.

She's your child, Lord. You promised to tattoo us on the palm of Your hand. You know that every day she becomes more precious to me. So, for both of us, I pray for Your protection and for Your guidance to help us find her. She is truly in the den of lions. Shut their mouths and give her deliverance. Thank You for Your promises.

Rick's praying was interrupted by the ringing of his cell phone.

Caller ID said it was his boss in Brunswick. "Larry," he called as he put the call on speaker. "Message from home."

"Yes, sir," he said into the phone.

"Rick, is Larry Robb with you?"

"Yes, sir. You're on speaker."

"Okay. Big news from our forensic auditors. Relay as much of this to your buddies in the Coast Guard as you think they will need. I assume you're still waiting for them."

"Yes, sir. We are."

"Okay. We've overestimated the importance of the targeting chips for the cash flow of the Onyx Group. It is a new and relatively small operation. The group's main enterprise is in the extracting of tantalum from the ground and the recovery of the metal from previously manufactured products."

"What in the world is tantalum?" Larry's question came just a moment before Rick could ask the same thing.

"When you get time, you can look it up on Wikipedia. But the short version is that it is a rare metal occurring and used in an alloy with another mineral. I won't bore you with the name. It has become extremely valuable recently for its use in the manufacture of electronic components and lab equipment. But the important fact is that one of the largest known deposits on earth has been found in northwestern part of the Kingdom of Arabia, which happens to be Al Masih's area of influence. If he could discover an inexpensive, feasible method of exploiting this valuable resource, he could move from being a minor prince in the royal family to closer to succession to the throne."

"And Blackstone's corporation would make that possible," Rick said.

"Good Lord," Larry said. "This is indeed a huge can of worms in the Arabian coffee. Aims is probably being held by White, the guy who stands to lose in a big way if Blackstone is not found and brought back into the execution of the plan."

Just then, the two investigators heard the sound of the Coast Guard chopper arriving.

"Here comes our ride," Rick said. "Do we share this information with Orbison and his buddy at the Coast Guard?"

"I think yes," Collier said. "They'll need to know some of this to prepare for what they are facing in this rescue operation. With so much to lose, your opponents are going to be willing to take huge risks. So watch your sixes. Bring back the commander. Keep me posted."

Rick and Larry grabbed their gear and headed toward the bright orange chopper waiting for them a few feet away. Orbison stood at the open door, reaching out a hand to help the two men aboard. Rick slipped his phone into his windbreaker before reaching for the chief petty officer's hand.

"Just got some news from Brunswick. We'll share it when we're airborne," he said.

Orbison was still connected to the chopper's intercom, and while Rick and Larry were securing themselves and plugging into the communications system, Orbison alerted the crew.

"Our two new guys have some intel. When we're in the air, they'll share."

When Orbison saw the power light on Rick's headset come on, he said, "Okay, marine, let's have it."

"Guys, our primary objective is the rescue of our missing Special Agent Commander Wallace. I'll leave out extraneous details, but our forensics team has found evidence that these guys could be Arabian. They're facing a big loss, and everyone's definitely desperate. They've already killed a couple of navy flag officers and their own pilot. The stakes are high, and they are ruthless. When we have time, we can share the details, but for now, time is of the essence, and we need to find and rescue Commander Wallace ASAP. We don't know how big a force we are facing and how much firepower they have. They've nothing more to lose."

Orbison's friend Davy Jones came on the line. "We're good, marine," he said. "This search and rescue team has SWAT training and gear. We're rated the best in the Florida Coast Guard. We'll have this."

"Awesome," Larry said. "I like working with the best of the best. That's why I'm on this team."

Orbison grinned. "Okay, Rick," he said. "You must have some questions."

"I do. Have you gotten a reading yet on Wallace's tracker frequency?"

"Just picked up a signal as we landed to pick you guys up. We're reading a heading of 170 degrees, true, and a range of less than twenty miles." Again, this was Davy Jones's voice.

"Sounds like Blackstone's Obsidian Haven Island," Orbison offered.

"My thinking too, Cliff," Jones said.

"Do we know exactly what structures are there?" Rick asked.

"This is what we mapped when we did our initial inspection," Jones said. "Take a look at the plasma back there."

What looked a small, flat-screen TV mounted on a bulkhead, lit up. It showed an aerial view of the island. Near the landward end of the dock stood a two-story structure wrapped with a wide veranda, with several small cabanas scattered nearby that backed up to a low rise that ran like a backbone the length of the island. Near what was surely the main house was a small outbuilding whose use or purpose had not been designated.

The entire eastern portion of the island was covered with sea grapes and palmetto foliage, but at the farthest point from the dock was a small clearing that was bordered by what looked like a sandy beach. The clearing was obviously man-made and showed the stakes and trenches for a possible concrete pour. Obviously, another structure was under construction.

"Didn't you say that White gave you the tour for your inspection, Chief?" Rick asked Orbison.

"Yeah. I did."

"Did you ask what these two outbuildings were to be used for?"

"Yeah. He said the one closest to the house was to be a utility structure to service the yacht and helicopter when it was there. He said there would be a helipad laid out next to it."

"What about this other one?"

"He said it was to be a dockin' place for neighbors who visited on their own yachts. When I asked him why it was so distant from the main structure, he said it was to ensure privacy for both the Blackstones and their visitors. At the time, that seemed to be plausible, but now I'm not so sure.

"Davy, do we got any recent satellite shots of this?" Orbison asked.

"Wait one. I'll look."

"Try to find a side angle shot," Orbison said. "Let's get an idea of what it looks like comin' in ta it by Zodiac."

"Good thinking, Chief," Rick said. "Since we'll be going in in the dark, we need to know what is there."

Just then, the view on the plasma screen changed, showing a low, virtually cube-shaped structure with foliage growing close. Facing the small beach was a door with only a small window in it. No utility lines were attached to the building, but there was a small enclosure nestled against the front of the building on the seaward side.

"What do you think, Cliff?" Jones asked. "Think that is a generator enclosure on the side?"

"Likely. Prob'ly necessary if the lack of windows means anythin'."

"Not only that," Rick said. "Makes the structure harder to breach."

"There's that," Orbison agreed.

"What do you think it is being used for now?" Rick's question seemed to kick everyone in the gut. None of their speculations made for pleasant scenarios.

"Cliff," Jones said, "we're approaching the island. We are activating all our infrared cameras and scanners. We'll be checking for heat sources inside the building as well as sentries outside. I'm going to run our take on the plasma."

"Okay, Davy," Orbison said. "Go fer it."

The helicopter descended and began a slow, counterclockwise turn around the target location as the plasma screen went dark and then bloomed with splotches of intense color. Davy Jones came back on the intercom.

"Cliff," he said. "I haven't heard from any of the members of the SWAT team. Are they awake?"

"Knock it off, Jones," the team leader said. "We might toss you out so you can find your locker on the bottom of the Gulf."

Larry snickered at the reference.

"Don't worry, Davy." Orbison chuckled. "They're payin' close attention ta the screen."

"Tell the cab driver once more 'round the block," Rick said. "I want another look at what we see before we go in."

When they had completed another circle, the pilot took them off a few miles to the southeast before putting them in a hover. Rick, Larry, Orbison, and the SWAT team were already conferring to fine-tune their plan of attack. The infrared scans showed two sentries outside the building and three warm bodies inside. All of the bodies appeared to be standing, except one inside the building.

"That's Aims," Rick said, pointing to the apparently prone blotch of color.

"Agreed," said Orbison and Larry.

"Okay," said the SWAT team leader, "we have four hostiles and one hostage." He tapped two of his men on the shoulder. "You two, take care of the sentries. Silently." The two designated team members nodded. He tapped the team member closest to him. "You use the battering ram and get the door open when the sentries are down."

"Okay, boss."

He turned to the other three, addressing his question to Orbison. "Which one of you three is the best shot?"

"The jarhead here," Orbison said. "He was a marine sniper back in the day. The Stringbean is a close second, bein' a deer and pig hunter."

"Okay. Chief," the team leader said, "can you handle getting the hostage out, while we three concentrate on the two bad guys in there?"

With their plan of attack clear and all of the raiders protected with body armor, they signaled the chopper crew to deploy the Zodiac and the rappel lines. Within minutes, the inflatable and raiders were cruising with silenced motor back to their target, which was only a mile or so away. On the run in, Rick was praying.

Okay, Lord, here we go. Prepare the way before us, in the presence of the enemy, please. Help us to be in time for Aims. Thank You, Lord.

They beached the Zodiac a few yards along the coast of the island, to the northeast. The team settled their night vision glasses into place, while the two assigned to take out the sentries slipped through the foliage. When the others saw the all-clear sign, they stepped to the door of the blocky building. At the nod from the team leader, the ram hit the door, and the others burst inside.

✦ ❧ ✦

Aims was staring at White and his sidekick when the door fell open and six men burst into the room, pushing up their night vision goggles as they came. She recognized Rick, Larry, and Orbison instantly. Rick and Orbison were immediately at her side as the other four surrounded her tormentors and subdued them.

When they had White and the others bound and gagged and Aims out of the building, the SWAT team leader contacted Jones in the chopper so they would meet them at the beached Zodiac.

Again, the lines came down, and the four captives, the three SWAT team members, and the four navy investigating team members were taken back on board the chopper, along with the now deflated Zodiac. The captives were immediately shackled to the walls of the chopper bay, and Aims was being examined by the Coast Guard medic as they began their trip back to the station at Fort Meyers Beach.

Chapter 10

The member of the SWAT team who was also a corpsman draped a blanket around Aims's shoulders and knelt in front of her. Rick seated himself beside her and wrapped an arm around her shoulders. His heart lifted in relief and praise that she seemed to be okay. After taking her blood pressure and listening to her heart and lungs, the medic took out a small penlight to check her pupils and how well she could track the light. He had her tip her head down so he could check the back of her head, where the kidnappers had clouted her. His touch was gentle but sure. He had obviously done this before—a lot of times. He also had her squeezing his fingers and resisting his pressure on her feet. Her knee jerked normally to the tapping of his small rubber-headed mallet.

"I haven't had a chance to thank you guys for coming for me. I was afraid things were going to get ugly, but your arrival prevented that."

"Just doing our job, ma'am." The medic grinned.

"That goes for you too, Rick," she said, leaning toward him to

Naomi L. Carter

apply gentle pressure to his chest. "You always seem to be close by when I'm in trouble or in pain."

"Or both—huh, Aims?" He grinned.

"My dad must have really done a number on you for you to make such a commitment to watching over me."

"My presence with you has absolutely nothing at all to do with your father." Although he was smiling, his eyes blazed with intensity. "It has even more to do with how much *I* need to be with you, rather than taking care of you. You've proven over and over that you can take care of yourself."

"Well, this time, when I came to, I knew there was nothing I could do for myself. I remembered your prayer before Larry and I went to interview Blackstone on the *Obsidian*. For once since I wiped out my fighter on the deck of the carrier, I felt like maybe God was with me and listening. That's why I could fall asleep until White and his goon came for me."

"Pardon me, ma'am," the corpsman said. "Did you say you fell asleep after waking from being unconscious?"

"Yes, I did," she replied.

"You're sure it was sleep and not a relapse into unconsciousness?"

"Yes," she said. "There was a refreshing, restful feeling to it, even if I was wakened by the sidekick ripping the duct tape from my eyes and mouth."

"Interesting," the medic said. "We always caution people about falling asleep after a concussive injury. But in your case, I think it may have had the effect of allowing your brain to recover from its injury. Much like a medically induced coma does. All my neurological tests indicate no injury to your brain. All of your responses indicate a normal, functioning brain. Of course, we won't be certain of that until we do an MRI on you at the infirmary on the station, but that nap, however long it was, seems to have been the best medicine for you. Amazing.

"Keep the blanket on her, marine," he said to Rick as he moved off to join his team.

Larry seated himself on the other side of Aims and leaned across her.

"I called Brunswick like you said, boss. Just got off the horn with Collier. He said not to worry about getting our chopper back. We're to spend the night with the Coasties at Fort Meyers Beach, and we'll sort the rest out in the morning."

"Okay, Larry, thanks," Rick said.

Now Orbison joined them.

"Update for ya."

"What now, Chief?" Aims asked. There was a trace of weariness in her tone.

"The Collier County Sheriff's office notified us that White filed a missin' person report on Blackstone and his wife yesterday afternoon. He said Aims and Larry were the last people to have seen them. Sheriff has the two of you listed as persons of interest in their disappearance."

"You're kidding," Larry said. "That little worm. Wait till I get my hands on him. I'd say that's classic pot calling the kettle black, given what he had engineered for Aims."

"Chill, Stringbean," Orbison said. "You both have an alibi. We'll get this sorted out in the mornin' too. Just thought y'all'd get a chuckle out of it."

"Cliff?" Davy Jones's voice came over the intercom. "We're

getting an unidentified tracking signal heading out across the Gulf. Looks like it might be headed for Cancun."

"Who's tracking it?" Larry asked.

"Signal is coming off the encrypted military communications satellite that's geostationary over Central America."

"Okay," Larry said. "I forgot to mention it, but I planted a tracker behind the used tire dock bumper in the boathouse enclosure of Blackstone's yacht before we left yesterday afternoon. Those Arabians aren't the only ones who can plant trackers. Looks like the Arab prince and his kids are bugging out and heading for home."

"Are we sure that he's takin' nothin' of strategic importance with him?" Orbison asked.

"No, we're not certain," Rick said. "But so far, all the evidence says that the only thing he probably retrieved from all this is Admiral Carter's briefcase. And we have Carter's own list of papers that he was taking with him. So we know what he's got."

"You know what bothers me in all this?" Aims inserted.

"No," Rick said, "but I'm sure you are going to tell us."

"Yes, I am," she said. "I keep hearing White sneering that 'the navy has no idea what this is all about.' It makes me worried that there is more here than we've discovered so far. I mean, what could we have missed? Will we have time to find out what it is?"

Her words dropped like heavy stones into a still pond. The team sat, as if mesmerized by the widening circles on the surface of the pond. Just before anyone could recover enough to speak, Aims felt the motion of the chopper shift and realized that they were descending to the Fort Meyers Beach Coast Guard Station. There was a lot of organized confusion, what with getting Aims to the infirmary to be checked out, prisoners to be secured in the station's brig, and emergency supplies to be restocked on the search and rescue chopper.

At last, the team met up in the comm center on the station to debrief their home office. Rick and Larry took the lead in updating the operations officers in Brunswick on the status of Aims and the team during the teleconference. She was just as happy to let them. When Rick reported that the MRI of Aims's head and upper spine revealed no complications from her rough treatment at the hands of White and his crew, Collier looked at Aims.

"You're uncharacteristically quiet, Agent Wallace. You okay?

"Yes, sir," she replied, her smile not very broad. "It's been a long day but nothing a good night's rest won't remedy. The medics told me that if I got six to eight hours of sleep, I'd be cleared to full duty. So I'm looking forward to that."

"Aims raised a question earlier, sir," Rick began. "I think we should fill her in with the information that you gave Larry and me just before we mounted our rescue operation. You know, about Blackstone's company and the rare metal."

"I am sure you can handle that, Rick," Collier replied. "We don't want to have that information floating in cyberspace any more than we need to."

"Good enough, sir. Maybe it will be just what we all need to help us sleep."

"I hope so. Are we all clear and on the same page?"

"Yes, sir. I think so."

"I'll be sending you a text in the morning. For now, all of you get some rest. Okay?"

"Copy that," Rick and the team agreed. "We're clear."

When the communications link was cut, Aims looked at Rick and Larry.

"You got some information about Blackstone's operation?"

"Yeah," Larry said. "But things happened so fast we didn't get to share it with you until just now."

"Besides that," Rick said, "we didn't want White to know what we know. Might make our questions to him more effective."

"Makes sense," she agreed. "How about you give me the condensed version as a bedtime story."

"You can do that, boss," Larry said. "I've got a date with a pillow and a rack." He ambled off toward the bunk rooms they had been shown earlier.

"Walk with me," Rick said. "We'll walk and talk so you can get some sleep sooner." He cupped her elbow with his hand, and they followed Larry out of the room.

"Okay, Rick," she said as they headed down the corridor, "what about Blackstone's company and this rare metal? I assume we are not talking about gold, silver, or platinum."

"You would be right." He smiled. "Again."

"So, what?"

"Collier said we should look it up on Wikipedia. But the short version is that it is rarer and more valuable than the three you mentioned. And it's in demand now because of its uses in the manufacture of electronic components and high-tech surgical instruments. It is called a conflict resource."

"Is that like blood diamonds?"

"Something like that. But right now it is important because the largest deposit most recently located is in the northwestern corner of Arabia, which is Al Masih's area of influence."

"Let me guess," Aims said. "Blackstone's company knows how to mine it or reclaim it."

"Right again."

"Worms in the Arabian coffee," Aims said.

"Almost an exact quote of Larry's reaction," Rick said. "Sound like it could be the missing piece of the puzzle?"

"Yeah." She sighed. "I'd think so. I don't know if I'll sleep better because it sounds like the key to the situation or if I'll sleep worse worrying about Blackstone and the implications of all this." By now they had reach reached the door to Aims's room.

Rick wrapped his arms around her and pressed her head against his shoulder. Encircled by his strength, hearing the steady beat of his heart against her ear, swamped her with a warm sense of safety. It fed a deep hunger she hadn't even been aware of, like finally coming home after too long an absence.

"You've been through a lot in the last few hours," he said. "And you've handled it like a trouper. I'm proud of you. I'm sure your folks would be too."

"I've had more help than I deserve. A presence when I was alone and helpless. I'm grateful for that."

"You prayed?"

"Yeah. And He answered."

Rick released her so he could search her face. Satisfied, Rick reached for her hand, saying, "Let's pray for rest for all of us tonight. Tomorrow could get dicey when we go to pick up the Bell chopper to take back to Brunswick. We need to be ready for anything, and we need to bring our A game."

Reaching for his hand, Aims said, "Yes, let's. Would you? My brain feels kind of battered."

"That's because it has been," Rick said. "But yes, I'll pray for us.

"Holy Spirit, our Advocate, thank You for surrounding us and keeping us safe. Thank You for helping us safely rescue Aims from White and his crew. Thank You for helping us gather information that clarifies what we are still dealing with. You know what we face tomorrow. We ask You to give our bodies and our spirits rest, reminding us in the small hours that You are with us and will be our present help in time of trouble. Prepare our hearts to be able to trust You for our safety and protection tomorrow. Thank You now for what you will do for us. In Jesus's name. Amen."

He pulled her into his arms for a moment, and she heard again the strong beat of his heart. Then he kissed her lightly on the forehead and released her.

"Sleep well, Aims."

Then he was gone, and she felt a little bereft as she entered her room and prepared for bed. As she removed her boots, she realized that she had performed this same ritual less than twelve hours ago on board the *Chameleon*. It felt like she had been up for days, and every joint and pin in her body ached. She remembered waking up in the concrete bunker on Obsidian Haven Island. How she had been swamped by regret that she would die before she had the chance to explore her feelings for Rick. Because she might love him. Then she remembered the peace that had wrapped her and let her sleep even in her captivity. She wished to experience that peace again. As her head settled into the pillow, she found herself giving thanks for Rick, the team, the Coast Guard, and her rescue. She promised herself that she would entertain the possibility that she and Rick could be more than best friends, the very next chance she got.

Rick settled into the chair beside the set of bunk beds. Larry lay on the bottom tier, his back to Rick, and the sound of his soft snores filled the silence. Rick's boots dropped beside his chair, and his hands paused in the process of preparing to climb into the upper bunk. His thoughts turned again to the woman whose side he had just left. What a strong, amazing person. How he had despaired of seeing her alive again when the hijacked chopper passed overhead and away into the dark. How he regretted allowing her to keep them at arm's length from each other. How he wanted to spend the rest of his life with her. To tell her he loved her. As he climbed up into bed, he sent a prayer upward. *Father, watch over us the rest of this night. Thank You for the second chance to express my love to Aims. Prepare the way for us, please.*

Chapter 11

Aims was wakened the next morning by knocking on her door.

"Aims, its Rick. Reveille. Coffee's waiting and a text message from home."

"Okay, okay, Rick. I'm awake. I'll be right there."

Aims rolled over and looked at her watch. *Wow. Nine o'clock. It's late. But I guess I needed it. Okay, let's do this. Coffee will help.*

When she entered the mess hall, she saw Rick and Larry sitting at a table with Orbison and another man, bending over an electronic tablet on the table. They all looked up and watched her approach. Holding her steaming coffee cup in front of her like a small, inadequate shield, she approached their table. Rick and Larry rose and held the only empty chair at the table, the one between theirs.

As she settled into her chair, Orbison greeted her.

"Aims, this is my Coastie buddy, Davy Jones. Davy, Aims Wallace. And she does too."

Jones grinned as he extended his hand.

"A pleasure, ma'am. I know. I have a quirky name too. My parents gave me mine. How did you get yours?"

"By beating the rest of my class in fighter pilot school during ground target training." She smiled.

"Wow, Aims," Larry said, looking at her face. "Halloween all over again. Cool."

When they saw Aims's face break into a grin, everyone laughed.

"Thanks, Larry," she said. "But I don't recommend the makeup artist. His methods are a little extreme. He gets no customer-satisfaction rating from me."

"Did the infirmary get documentation of your injuries?" Rick asked.

"Yes," she said. "They did the whole infrared shots, measurements routine for charges of aggravated assault. If you think it looks awesome now, wait until they start to turn green and yellow.

"So, what was so interesting that you were all staring at this tablet?" She gestured to the device lying on the table in front of them.

"This is the text message from home I mentioned," Rick said.

The others pushed the device closer to Aims so she could read it. It was a long text from their supervisor, Collier, in Brunswick, which Aims scanned. When she finished, she said, "Okay, let me see if I have the main points right.

"First, these guys we picked up are to be investigated, charged, and prosecuted in federal court here in southwest Florida. To facilitate that prosecution, Brunswick will forward back to us ballistic and forensic evidence, as well as the autopsy reports. NTSB will complete the examination of the plane wreckage at the base there and forward their report to the federal prosecutor's office here. The navy will add charges of murder of the two officers on the plane, as well as the kidnapping and assault charges from last night to the list of charges against them.

"Second, we are to remain in the area in order to assist the federal investigators as they continue to investigate these guys to see what other local support they have had in this endeavor. In addition, we are to locate and assist Blackstone in whatever way necessary for him to find out what has been going on within his company. We are to provide any security and protection he may require. Did I miss anything?"

Davy Jones looked at Orbison. "You're right, Cliff. She does aim. And she hits what she aims at."

Rick and Larry grinned at the other two men before Rick turned to Aims. "You nailed it," he said.

"Thanks, team leader. But now that we have our marching orders, what are our next steps? Looks to me like we have a lot of tasks to perform, and I want to know how we're going to prioritize them." She and Larry took out their electronic notepads.

"Okay," said Larry, writing as he talked. "We have prisoners to interrogate and to turn over to the federal marshals. And we need to get back to our wheels at Uncle Orbison's marina."

Orbison cocked an eyebrow at Larry's honorific title but made no comment.

"Speaking of which," Rick said. "Chief, what is the condition of the *Chameleon*?"

"Other than bullet holes in the superstructure," Orbison said, "she's in pretty fair shape. Like I suspected, the low-impact torpedo struck the housin' of the retractable counter board, which we made to be a piece of armor, so the keel wasn't breached. Bullet holes in bulkheads are not a problem. Easy to patch. They don't bleed." He grinned at them. "I guess what I'm saying is she's good to go, and I planned to take her back to her berth at what you guys called the parkin' lot. Am I still under contract as a security guy?"

"Without a doubt," Rick responded.

"Does he need any backup?" Davy Jones inquired.

"That's not a bad idea," Rick replied. "But he's a private contractor. You'll have to apply to him for the position, if he thinks it's necessary."

"I have a question," Aims said. "If the *Obsidian* is headed for Cancun, when will she arrive?"

"Depends on when she headed that way," Jones said, "and from where, as well as her speed, but I'd guess she'll get there sometime right after daybreak tomorrow."

"Does anybody think that the Blackstones might have gone underground on board their own yacht?" Aims said. "That idea just occurred to me."

"Whoa," said Orbison. "Now that's a novel idea. You know, if the captain and crew of that boat were loyal to Blackstone instead of Al Masih, as I always figured, that would be a very viable option for them."

"So," Aims continued, "when Al Masih and the twins disembark at Cancun, which I assume they will, then the captain can provision, refuel, and head back this way. From what we saw on our visit, wouldn't you say that Art Blackstone could search what's been going on at his corporation remotely, Larry? I thought he might have the technical tools already on board, so if he had a secure place to hide and a computer terminal, he could already have made a big dent in finding out what he needs to know."

"Yeah," Larry replied. "I think he could do that easily

enough—especially if he had some trusted employees on the inside of the corporate headquarters to help with his searches."

"Then we could expect some sort of notification from them as early as tomorrow," Aims said. "That could add some dimension to our questioning of White. Right, Rick?"

"Yeah," he said. "Good thought. Now back to our to-do list. Transportation.

"Our little chopper should be okay where it is on Obsidian Haven Island for the moment. Don't you think, Chief?"

"Don't see why not. Right now, we think the island is deserted. So as long as it's securely tied down, it should be okay. If Davy wants to come with me when I take the *Chameleon* home, we can check it out on the way."

"Good," Rick said. "While you're checking it out, Larry and I tossed our duffels onto the chopper. Maybe you could pick them up for us and we can get them back when you bring the *Maisie Mae* home."

"Mine too," said Aims. "Can you get that done by the close of business today?"

"Affirmative," Orbison said. "Since you don't need us to deal with interrogation, Davy and I'll head out now."

"Okay," Rick said. "But before you go, can you make arrangements for us to get a ride back to the marina, where our rental wheels are parked, when we're through here?"

"Sure thing," Jones said. "On my way out to the boat."

"So," Rick continued, "priority one is the interrogation of our prisoners so we can begin to outline evidence for the charges against them as they pertain to the deaths of two navy guys, the attack of a federal officer, and acts of domestic terrorism. Not to mention murder of the civilian pilot."

The team nodded in agreement. As they rose from the table and headed toward the interrogation rooms, they were still talking between themselves.

"I think the first thing I want to know is if there are any more bad guys hiding out in the bushes around here," Larry said. "I'm not interested in being a target for any more stragglers.

"So, I think we should observe them in isolation for a time to determine who is the most likely to talk. They've been kept separate from each other since we brought them here."

The hours that followed were almost as grueling for Aims as the beating they had given her. While she and Larry faced White's three accomplices, Rick went one-on-one with White, who had never interacted verbally with him before. When the US marshals came to escort the four men to the federal lockup in downtown Fort Meyers, the navy investigators each breathed a silent sigh of relief. They gathered in the mess hall before meeting their Coast Guard driver who would take them back to their rented lodgings at Orbison's marina. After they ate and stared into their coffee in silence for several long moments, Rick stirred.

"Did we get anything?"

"Not much," Larry said. "A lot of sinister stares and anti-American ranting. You?"

"It took a while," Rick said. "I'm glad you shared what Art Blackstone told you about the interaction between White and Art's mom. That's what finally shook things loose. It took figuratively bringing her into the room to sit at the table, watching him; that got White to begin talking. We have a long way to go, but I think we found the first chink in his armor."

"I don't think the others are going to yield much until we begin to get some sort of admission from White," Aims said. "This is just the start of some intense interrogation."

"Larry," said Rick, "you were concerned about some stragglers floating around out there. Did you or Aims pick up any indication that that was indeed the case?"

Larry and Aims looked at each other before Aims replied. "Not really. Our session was a textbook example of hitting a brick wall. In fact, beating our heads against that wall. No matter how we phrased our questions, we got a lot of words but no information. I'm thinking we need to take a break from all the drama, get back to the *Lindy Lou* for some rest, and give White and his cohorts a chance to contemplate their belly buttons behind bars for a while."

"Sounds like a plan," said Rick. "Let's do that."

The team got back to the *Lindy Lou* before Orbison returned from the boathouse, where he exchanged his transport from the *Chameleon* to the *Maisie Mae*. When he delivered their duffels, he found Larry and Rick at their laptops, and they told him that Aims was taking some downtime in her cabin. Larry was using the laptop to get the background on tantalum that Collier had suggested would help them know exactly what was involved in the Arabian coffee worms, so they would have an idea of how proceed. Rick was giving an update on their activities.

After a few moments of small talk, the men agreed that Orbison would take Aims and Rick to the Obsidian Haven Island to retrieve the chopper the next day, while Larry drove the rented Escalade to the airport to meet them, getting the team and their transport back together in one place.

The recovery of their hijacked helicopter from Obsidian Haven was almost anticlimactic. No one was around the few outbuildings, and the *Obsidian* slip was empty. Aims and Rick checked over the small helicopter, but it had not been sabotaged. After running her preflight check, they boarded the small rotary wing craft, and Aims fired it up. Rick occupied the copilot position.

As she flew away from the island, Aims wondered where Blackstone and his wife were. It seemed to be a natural thing to breathe a prayer for their safety, if, indeed, he was what he claimed to be—a patriot betrayed by a childhood friend. And if not, then let them be brought to justice. So many people had been hurt by what happened.

They were pulling into the parking area at the marina when Aims was surprised by the comm link in her ear coming to life.

"Commander," Collier said from the office in Brunswick, Georgia. "What is your present position?"

"We're just arriving back at the marina to our rented boat lodgings. What's up, sir?" she asked.

"First tell me where your prisoners are."

"They are in the federal lockup in Fort Meyers Beach, while we and the federal prosecutor's office continue to gather information."

"Is Rick up on this link?"

"I'm here, boss," Rick replied into his throat mic.

"Remember the communication we had earlier from the Arabian coffee drinker?"

"Yes, sir." Rick and Aims exchanged glances.

"We just got another message to forward to you. 'Arabian worms eradicated from Obsidian. We're up for air. Can meet you at the Haven, day after tomorrow morning, if okay. Would like to give you some onyx pearls.' So do you want to change your plans and meet there?"

"What is the *Obsidian*'s current position, according to the locator Larry planted?" Rick asked.

"They are moored at the harbor at Cancun. According to the harbormaster, they are scheduled to head back to Naples in the morning. Three passengers transferred from the yacht to the airport of Cancun."

Rick and Aims exchanged another glance.

"Do you think Art and Alexa Blackstone were hidden aboard the yacht the whole time?" The audacity of that idea was giving her some trouble, even though she had first suggested it.

"I wouldn't put it past them," Rick observed.

"I'm waiting for an answer here, guys. What do you want to do with this?" Collier's words sounded more impatient than his tone of voice.

"Let them know that we'll meet them when they arrive on Obsidian Haven. In the meantime, we'll keep you in the loop," Rick said.

❦

It was an awesome sight to watch the huge yacht coast to a gentle stop at the long pier at Obsidian Haven Island. Aims and the team had just disembarked from the Zodiac on which Orbison had delivered them when the yacht's nose appeared between the clumps of sea grapes bordering the channel from the Gulf. It was obvious that the yacht's crew had performed similar operations frequently because there was not a glitch in the whole procedure. While Larry and Aims watched, Rick and Orbison waited on the pier to catch the mooring lines tossed from the deckhands. A gangway was extended, which Rick secured to the pier. Art and Alexa Blackstone came to its head, waiting to welcome their guests.

Rick led the team up the ramp.

"Good morning, Mrs. Blackstone, Mr. Blackstone," he said, extending his hand to each of them. "I'm Special Agent Rick Holt, and I work with Commander Wallace and Agent Larry Robb. We have firefighter Cliff Orbison with us. He's our security guy and landlord while we're here in the Naples area."

"Good morning, Agent Holt and Mr. Orbison," Art Blackstone replied. "My captain says you two handle lines like professionals. He says if either or both of you want a job, he'll hire you."

"Thank you, sir." Rick grinned. "I've done this a few times. My uncle was a riverboat captain on the Mississippi. Orbison here was a former navy chief petty officer. So, you see, we're both showing off old skills."

"You both were taught well. Then again, you do it like you liked the job, which makes good teachers look even better.

"Hello, again, Aims, Larry. Good to see you again. It looks like you ran into some trouble, Aims."

"It wasn't as bad as it could have been," Aims said. "Rick and Larry came to my rescue before things got too bad. I've just been wearing some very different colors of makeup for a few days. Nothing to worry about." Alexa Blackstone's hand brushed Aims's arm in sympathy.

"Mr. Orbison," said Alexa, "Agent Holt said you were a firefighter. At which fire station do you work?"

"I'm stationed right up the road from your estate. Just north of the executive airport."

"Mr. Orbison was one of the first responders to the crash of your plane the other day," Aims said. "It was his astute observation of the rank of your passenger, Admiral Carter, that got us involved in this investigation in the first place."

Art Blackstone extended his hand. "Thank you, sir. I'm glad you were so observant. If you had not been, we might have been in severely different circumstances and been oblivious of the danger. As soon as my captain finishes delegating mooring tasks, he will be joining us up on our observation space. There is morning coffee, along with juice and rolls awaiting us there."

"American coffee, sir?" Larry asked.

"Definitely American." Art Blackstone chuckled.

Art and Alexa Blackstone led their guests up a series of steps to a shaded seating area. It was furnished with deck chairs and accompanying side tables arranged in a manner which that make for easy flow of conversation between its occupants. It afforded a near-panoramic view of their surroundings, including a glimpse of the Gulf beyond the break in the sea grapes to the west. Each of them helped themselves to the refreshments arrayed on the buffet bar before settling into their seats.

"So, Mr. Blackstone ..."

"Art, please, Agent Holt," Blackstone interrupted "Please call me Art. I'm more comfortable with that."

"Okay, Art. Tell me, were you and your wife hiding out on board here this whole time?"

"Yes. In the years when White and I had to resist the pressures to join warring neighborhood gangs, I made it a practice to never enter a situation without knowing where the exits were. I had a place in the engine room, and Alexa joined the cabin maintenance crew. It's true that no one notices those who serve them. The only person who was aware of our presence was our captain."

As if on cue, the yacht captain appeared at the head of the companionway and joined the group.

"Ah, here is the captain now. Folks, please meet my college buddy, Gabe Jeffrys."

While Art performed the introductions to the yacht captain, Aims palmed her phone and snapped a surreptitious shot of his face. She had been shocked to recognize his face from the internet photos of the Al Masih entourage, although the name Art gave was not the name listed in the caption to the photo. She wanted to have a shot for comparison and for a facial recognition check. She fought to keep the blast of cold growing inside from showing on her own face, so she left Rick, Larry, and Orbison to carry the conversational ball, contributing as little as necessary to the easy banter. As she should have anticipated, Rick soon noticed her low level of interaction. He glanced at her and lifted a brow. She gave an imperceptible shake of her head.

At the next break in the flow of small talk, Rick turned to Art.

"I think I heard one of the team members mention that you had some knowledge of onyx pearls. I'm curious about that. Sounds intriguing."

"Yes, I believe I did promise to do some research on this rarity." He reached into a shirt pocket and withdrew a thumb drive. "I collected it on this so you would have all of my research, easily accessible." He handed it across to Rick, who pocketed it and rose.

"We've taken up enough of your time. I'm sure you have a lot of loose ends to tie up in the wake of White's alleged acts of betrayal. And we still have some loose ends of our own to clear up in our investigation of your plane's crash. So, if you all are ready, team, let us take our leave of this delightful company and get back to the job.

"It was not until the Zodiac, on which Orbison had ferried them to the island, was out of sight of the *Obsidian* and Larry had completed a sweep of the boat to ensure there was no electronic enhancement to its structure that Aims felt the tension in her shoulders ease. While she knew there could still be an invisible bull's-eye centered between her shoulder blades, she thought she could at least draw a breath or two and share her concerns with the others so she would not be the only one aware of their danger.

"All right, Aims," Rick said as they stepped onto the dock, heading for the *Maisie Mae*. "Spill."

Orbison and Larry stopped dead in their tracks and stared at the two of them.

On the ride in, Aims had thumbed through her phone's picture gallery and located the shot of the entourage of the Arabian prince that she had discovered prior to the first visit with Art Blackstone. She held out her phone so Rick could see the photo, then tapped a face in the group shot.

"Look familiar?" she asked. Rick and the others leaned closer to see.

"Oh, wow," Larry said. "It's the captain, Gabe Jeffrys. Good catch, Skipper."

"What name's on the caption of this photo?" Orbison asked.

"Avram Ehrens," Aims said. "We should do backgrounds on both names."

"What bothers me," said Orbison, "is the fact that we could be lookin' at two groups after the same thing."

"Or we have an intelligence op being run to keep an eye on either Al Masih or Blackstone," Larry said.

"Or both," Rick observed.

"How on earth do y'all keep all these angles straight?" Orbison said, shaking his head.

"Not easy, Chief," Aims said. "This whole case has been a tangled web. Woven to deceive."

"Well, you're right, Aims," Rick said. "We're going to have to run both names for the captain. It's time we started pulling on some of these tangled threads and got to the bottom of this mystery."

"I'd like to see what Blackstone put together in his onyx pearls file," Larry said. "It might give us some clues we need to solve this whole thing."

"Good idea, Stringbean," Orbison said. "Let's chew on what we have before we ask for another servin'." He turned and led the team over to the *Maisie Mae.*

Chapter 12

Background checks were a boring and painstaking task. I[n] to be good at it, a person had to like digging through tons of [...] discover one nugget of fact. It always surprised Aims that L[...] ordinarily action-oriented person, was so good at ferreting [...] nuggets they needed. It was he who discovered the key to [...] out who Gabe Jeffrys was. He had taken Art Blackstone at [...] and began with the University of Florida yearbooks to see if [...] locate Jeffrys's picture along with Blackstone's and White's[...]

While he was following that bread crumb trail, Rick a[...] were examining the files on the thumb drive they receiv[...] Art Blackstone. True to his word, he had provided the pa[...] generated by the Onyx Group that detailed the histor[...] company's participation in providing the targeting chip[...] smart weaponry being used in the eastern Mediterranea[n] verbal instructions had been given to staff members, they [...] notes of those instructions, and there followed the docur[...] of their actions in carrying out those instructions. In alm[...]

case, the instructions and communications had originated over t signature of B. White, assistant to A. Blackstone, CEO.

"Well," said Rick, leaning back away from the computer screen. "This is one part of this investigation that is leading in a straight path to a smoking gun in the hands of White. That reminds me. I wonder what luck, if any, the US marshals are having in doing backgrounders on the three hoodlums we arrested with White."

"Let's call them and see," Aims said.

"Okay," Rick said. "I'll do that while you keep this up for a while. Okay?" At Aims's nod, he took his cell phone out onto the deck of the *Maisie Mae* and called the marshal's office.

When he returned a few moments later, he said, "Well, we have found another trail leading to some solid information."

"What is that?" Aims inquired, rubbing her eyes as she looked up at him.

"Fingerprints of White's three cohorts revealed the identities of three enforcers for a drug cartel operating in the West Miami area. Seems that White kept his connections with them away from Blackstone, insisting that he had escaped that element of their high school days. When the identities came back, some smart guy in that office decided to separate the three. Each one of them was given the information that their names and gang affiliations were known and that one of their friends was ready to roll over on them and make a deal. They began to sing in three-part harmony, and they had no qualms about implicating White as the brains behind their activities in the Marco Island plane takedown."

"I was just thinking about what you said about White loosening up when you mentioned Blackstone's mother. What was that?"

"I've thought about that myself," Rick said. "I think it was an

attempt to play a head game with me. Some of those gang members are so convinced of their superior intelligence that they believe they can con anyone, especially law enforcement. At any rate, whatever it might have been, he hasn't provided any useful information."

Larry said, "All right. Now we're talking."

Rick and Aims turned toward him as he looked up from his computer screen.

"Seems that White wasn't the only one keeping his college friendships a secret. Art Blackstone met both his yacht captain and his wife while he was in college, and while White met and interacted with Alexa, he never met or dealt with Jeffrys at all. That was how Jeffrys pulled off the dual-name thing with White. Blackstone and Alexa must have known what it was all about and never said anything."

"Well," said Aims, "what *was* it all about?"

"I'll put it up on the plasma," Larry said. "I was doing a routine backgrounder on Gabe Jeffrys when I noticed his recruitment information by an organization I knew to be a Defense Intelligence Agency front."

"How did you know that?" Rick asked.

"Because they tried to recruit me when I was approaching graduation, and I checked them out."

Rick and Aims rolled their eyes at each other.

"Anyway," Larry continued, "I got Collier to get me permission to search their database for Jeffrys, and I just hit pay dirt."

"First of all," Aims said, "what in Jeffrys's backgrounder tipped you off? Why did this front organization seek him out in the first place?"

"Okay," Larry said. "Look at his family history. Although

Gabe is a second-generation native-born American, his paternal grandparents emigrated from Damascus in the early nineteen hundreds. Gabe's father was raised bicultural, and so was Gabe. He speaks Arabic like a native.

"Art Blackstone met him and Alexa in some of his classes while studying metallurgy and international marketing. Jeffrys's university major was international trade relations, with a specialization in the Middle East. It was like he was tailor made to be inserted into Al Masih's household. Given that his family had been part of the yacht club society, what other position would they choose?

"So now, you see the dossier that DIA prepared for Gabe Jeffrys, a.k.a. Avram Ehrens."

The plasma screen showed education, work history, and yacht certifications granted to Avram Ehrens by the Arabic kingdom, in addition to birth certificate and other items that the intelligence community called pocket litter.

"So Art and Alexa would know of his recruitment by the Defense Intelligence Agency and his assignment to the Al Masih household?" Aims asked.

"Well, they didn't know about the details. All they knew was that he had taken employment overseas and was out of touch for several years. Jeffrys clued them to not speak about their prior relationship when he showed up with the *Obsidian*, which Al Masih presented to Blackstone as a gift to further his bid to become an investor in the Onyx Group's rare metal operations. There were few overlaps for Jeffrys to worry about, and Al Masih never spent a lot of time stateside."

"Wow," said Rick. "I think we need another face-to-face with those guys to nail down some of the specifics."

"Probably," Aims said. "Larry, does SECNAV know all this? Does Collier?"

"Not sure," he replied. "I'm forwarding it back to Collier to disseminate as he chooses. I think you're right, Rick. We need to be sure that there were no other accessories provided along with the yacht that might be reporting back to Al Masih."

"So, that is high on our to-do list," Rick said. "Along with digging around in White's associations while he was stopping communications from the Pentagon."

By now, it was late afternoon, and Orbison had been otherwise occupied while the team mined the internet. Now he poked his head into the salon from the galley. The appearance of his smiling face was accompanied by delicious smells of cooked food.

"Anyone hungry?"

"Me," responded Larry.

"Expected as much, Stringbean," the former navy chief said, chuckling.

When the team gathered around the breakfast bar, they saw Orbison's daughter, Maisie, helping him put out the food before they both joined them.

"Hope you folks don't mind," Orbison said, "but Maisie often joins me, and she wanted to get a closer look at this former navy fighter jock on your team."

"Don't mind at all, Chief," Aims responded. "Nice to have another woman in the mix. Sometimes I need something to dilute the testosterone. Do you find that to be true, Maisie?"

"Yeah, I do," she responded. "Dad keeps telling me that the military is now thoroughly coed, but I sometimes get the feeling that's more of a PR gimmick than actual fact."

"We've got a couple of sisters on the Joint Chiefs," Aims responded, "and a lady admiral in the navy."

"That rank your goal, Commander?" Orbison asked.

"Not really," she replied. "I just keep reupping because I've been unable to figure out what I'd do if I got out. I guess I've been so busy recovering from the crash of my fighter and then switching from a career of practicing law to investigating the crimes being committed to give it much thought.

"You know, marine," Orbison said, pointing at Rick, "I never figured you for slow, but I'd say you must have missed some signals somewhere along the way. I think the lady could be persuaded to consider another option, if it were offered."

"Put away your bow, Cupid," Aims said. "I want to ask Maisie about her friend who's a golf pro."

"What about him?" Maisie sounded suddenly wary.

"Well," Aims said, "Chief here reported that your friend was giving golf lessons to a couple of young men from the Middle East, as guests of Mrs. Blackstone."

"Yeah, he was," she said.

"Did you ever see them at the golf club where your friend works?"

"Now that you mention it," she said, "I did."

"I'd be interested in your take on the interaction between hostess and guests, from a woman's point of view."

"You mean Sam said she was all flirty and making moves on the young men, and did I see that as well?"

"You know, Chief," Aims said to Orbison, "you have one very sharp daughter. That's exactly what I am asking, Maisie. Did you see that in their interaction?"

"There was a lot of flirty interaction between the three," Maisie said. "But I think it was more wishful thinking on the part of the young men, and Mrs. Blackstone was too gracious to confront them directly. I never saw her initiate any of that type of playfulness."

"How did you come to ask that question, Aims?" Rick said.

"Tell me, Rick, did you see any indication in Alexa Blackstone's behavior that would lead you to believe that she would behave like a predator? I believe the term is as a cougar."

"I know my dad does not approve of most of the guys I date," Maisie interrupted. "But his opinion of Sam is right on. I wouldn't tell him that, and I only go out with Sam to pull my dad's chain, but I don't usually take Sam's name-dropping and evaluations of other people without large measures of salt." She looked over at her dad and stuck out her tongue. "Don't let that go to your head, Dad."

During the general laughter, Aims leaned toward Orbison. "Don't dare her to defy you, Chief. She's got a good head on her, and you did well with her. Left alone, she'll make good choices."

"Ya think?"

Aims nodded.

As the laughter subsided, Larry suddenly tapped on the countertop. "*That's* what's been bothering me about our interviews with the Blackstones. That discrepancy between what the chief was told about Mrs. Blackstone's response to the young twins and the interaction between Art Blackstone and Alexa that we observed. That bothered you too, Skipper, didn't it?"

"It did."

"Maisie," Aims went on, "whose idea was it for you to join us for dinner this evening?"

"Dad's," said Maisie.

"Do you suppose he really has respect for your opinions and he wanted you to give us a woman's take on the interaction between Mrs. Blackstone and the twins? In order to help us check out this difference?"

Maisie turned again toward her dad, her eyes narrowed speculatively. "You sly old fox. I think I've been underestimating you all my life."

"I think," Rick commented, "that the Orbison family is richly endowed with brain matter. Both of you are extremely good at what you do and should feel at ease with the roles you both play in the grand scheme of things."

"Well," said Larry, "I guess we can check off that little problem from the list. Now all we have to do is see if there are any more loose ends in the Blackstone household. Then we can turn over the investigation into White's possible other cohorts in the Naples area to the marshals. They can do their own preparation of the case against him while we head back to Brunswick."

They all rose from the table.

"Come on, Maisie," Aims said. "Let me help you do cleanup while the guys discuss fishing."

"Right," Maisie agreed. "I could do with some girl talk."

"So, Commander—"

"Please, Maisie," Aims interrupted. "Call me Aims."

"Okay," Maisie said as she put warm dishwater into the galley sink. "How long have you and the marine been a couple?"

"We're not a couple," Aims protested. "We're best friends and coworkers."

"You keep telling yourself that, you might miss out on something special. I've seen the way he looks at you. And, for that matter, the way you look at him.

"So, how long?"

"We've been friends since I woke up in Bethesda Naval Hospital several years ago. I wiped out my fighter on the flight deck in the Med, trying to make a night landing on the carrier. Rick came to check on me for my dad. He kept coming to walk me through rehab. We became best friends then and have been ever since."

"Let me get this straight," Maisie said. "You crashed your fighter?"

"Yeah. Messed myself up pretty well too."

"How did checking on you for your dad come about?"

"Well, Rick was attending LSU School of Law on the GI Bill and was interning in my dad's law office. My dad is a lot like your dad. Except my mom was in the picture too. My dad wasn't a military man, but he was a strict authoritarian. That's why I recognized a lot of the dynamics going on with you and your dad.

"Anyway, Dad was a pretty big-time lawyer in the state attorney's office and was in the middle of a big case. So, he couldn't come to check on me himself. He sent Rick in his place."

"You mean your dad cares about you, and he wants to keep close tabs on you."

"I suppose that's pretty accurate. See? We have similar family histories."

"Okay. But let's get back to you and Rick. Your dad sent him to check on you. Then what?"

"Well, for some reason, he kept coming back on the weekends. Ended up staying with me through rehab. Followed me into navy investigations."

"Did you ask him why he kept coming back?"

"Yeah, I did. He said he wanted to find out how tough I was. Kept challenging me to take the next step. Get to the next level."

"Can't resist a challenge either, can you?" Maisie grinned at her.

"Guess not. But Rick's a marine. If we were in a closer relationship than the one we have, I'm afraid he would treat me with the same controlling attitude. You know, like my dad treats my mother. Maybe like your dad treats you."

"No," said Maisie thoughtfully. "Actually, I don't see that in Rick. I see him waiting to see if you're going to wimp out. My dad's first expectation is that I will wimp out. I think Rick would be surprised if you did. I think Dad is always surprised when I don't. Your dad too?"

"Yeah. Now that you mention it. I hadn't thought about that before." Aims realized the difference was subtle but significant. At least to her. She'd have to think more about that. Maybe there wasn't as much of a barrier to letting Rick know how she felt as she'd been thinking there was. *Hmm.*

"Come on," said Maisie. "We're done here."

Soon after that, the investigators retreated to their space aboard the *Lindy Lou*, leaving the Orbisons to their own devices.

Larry ensconced himself in the small salon with his laptop, while Rick and Aims settled themselves on the long bench that lined three sides of the rear cockpit, watching the cloud formations in the sky as the evening deepened into night.

"Doesn't seem possible that it was only a few hours ago that I wondered if I would ever have a chance to enjoy such a view with you again," Rick said.

"I know. I thought the same thing."

"I had some regrets about that."

"I did too. What did you regret?"

After a stretch of silence, he eyed her and said with a small smile, "I'll tell you mine if you'll tell me yours."

"That sounds fair." Aims's smile matched his.

Rick drew in a breath to speak when several things happened at once.

Chapter 13

First came Orbison's shout from the fantail of the *Maisie Mae*.

"Vault!" he roared.

Next came Larry's shout from the salon of the *Lindy Lou*.

"Vault, guys!"

The three team members headed pell-mell down the companionway to the safe room at the prow. As Rick dogged down the latch, Larry moved to the wall with the monitor screens and gauges, which all came alive along with the red battle lantern mounted in the ceiling. One of the screens revealed an unmanned aerial vehicle, armed with a missile, skimming low over the water leading to the entrance of the marina. Another screen revealed a two-man submarine hugging the sea bottom of a waterway. While the three of them watched, they saw an air-to-air missile homing in on the unmanned vehicle, and then the screen bloomed with light and fell dark. At almost the same moment, the submarine seemed to move toward what looked like an oil drum that had dropped into the water just ahead of its path. That screen also bloomed with the light of the explosion and then fell dark.

The three of them were still staring at the blank screens when there was a banging at the door.

"Commander? Rick? Stringbean? Y'all okay?"

Rick released the hatch seal and opened the door to reveal Orbison standing in the corridor. As the light streamed in, the red lamp went out.

"Everyone okay?" Orbison asked again.

"What was all that?" Aims's insides were still quivering, but she was surprised by how calm her voice sounded. "That looked like some weird action videos. What happened?"

"That was our guardian angels on the job." Orbison grinned.

"Say what, Chief?" Larry asked.

"While you guys were searching cyberspace, I got a notification from my friend Davy Jones. SECNAV had arranged overwatch surveillance of our marina, which began when y'all returned from your interrogations at the marshals' office in Fort Meyers Beach. A high BARCAP was set up above us, an' a cutter was moored in the foliage beyond the perimeter of the marina. A trip wire was set, and if any threat, either from the air or underwater or both, crossed that line, it was to be taken out with extreme prejudice. I didn't get a chance to let you know before.

"The BARCAP took out the attackin' drone with an air-to-air missile, and the two-man sub was taken out by a single well-placed depth charge. Quick, clean, and no alarms for the civilians nearby. And no collateral damage. Your tax dollars at work."

"Will the US marshals be looking for whoever set this up?" Rick asked.

"The first investigation starts with the county sheriff's office," Orbison said. "Coast Guard will be notifying them of their actions, and they will be informed that this is part of a case that the marshals are working right now. Coast Guard is also notifying your boss in Georgia, as well as SECNAV, who authorized the action to be taken."

"Well," said Larry, "that checks off another box. We now know that there were some stragglers waiting in the bushes. And we still don't know how many, if any, more there still are. So, we still have work to do in the morning."

"And I guess," said Rick, "it's time to sound 'Taps.'"

Aims went to bed feeling like she was still holding her breath. It took a long time to corral her thoughts and feelings about the aborted conversation with Rick. What had he been about to say? Would there ever be an opportunity for her to find out? Would there ever be an opportunity for her to tell him that she loved him? Because she was sure now that she did.

❦ ⁂ ❦

The three team members sat over morning coffee, trying to block out an agenda for the day. Rick's cell chirped, signaling an incoming text message. He read it and then held it out for the others.

Overwatch reports yacht *Obsidian* currently moored outside Blackstone estate, Marco Island. No surviving raiders last night.

"That makes Art and Alexa Blackstone and Gabe Jeffrys more accessible to us," Larry observed.

"Ahoy, the *Lindy Lou*. Permission to board."

"Come ahead, Chief," Rick called. "Just making plans for the day."

"Did you get the report from overwatch?" Orbison asked as he joined them at the breakfast bar. He had brought his coffee mug, already steaming, with him.

"Larry just noted that the Blackstones would be easier for us to talk to this morning," Aims said. "Do you think we need to take our security with us?"

"My mamma used to say better to have it and not need it than need it and not have it, while she shoved the umbrella into my hand," Orbison said.

"Sounds like you'd like to ride along." Rick grinned.

"I think I'd feel better knowing you were with us," Aims said.

"I been thinkin'," Orbison said. "Did anyone do any checkin' of the list of employees that White supplied right after the crash? And did that list include any of the company employees from the Onyx Group plant?"

"We forwarded that list to Brunswick, but things have been moving so fast I haven't had time to check on whatever results may have been found," Rick said.

"Good catch, Chief," Aims said. "Let's check in with the home office and see what they found. Shall we get it sent to your plasma screen on the *Maisie Mae*?"

"Yeah," Orbison said. "Let's move this meetin' over there. Coffee's better over there anyway."

The four of them were settled in the salon of the *Maisie Mae* when the response to their inquiry arrived via a burst from the geostationary military encrypted satellite. It bloomed onto the large plasma screen, and Larry began manipulating it to separate it into its components so they could study them.

The first folder was the background information gathered on the Blackstone household staff. Their priority of scrutiny began with the place of birth. The Arabic name, Avram Ehrens, of the yacht captain jumped out at them, so he was their first subject to study.

What they found verified what information they already had; a good DIA agent, highly valued, intel product graded highly across all measured aspects, considered a highly effective operative.

"Aims," Rick said, "fire up your laptop. Let's see what is known about Gabe Jeffrys. I want to know what kind of clay this piece of art is made of."

"Already on it," she said. "Look at this academic record."

"I'm impressed by this notation," Larry said. "Admitted to MENSA. Look at that IQ. He's got eight points on me, and I've always been considered in the top 1 percent of the top 1 percent. Impressive."

"Okay," Rick said. "Let's look at what this tells us about his time with the Al Masih family."

"Looks like he joined Al Masih's entourage when the Arabian purchased his first yacht, christened *Arabian Treasure*. Avram Ehrens oversaw its construction, conducted its shakedown cruise, and has been its only captain. When Al Masih purchased it, the broker recommended that he hire Ehrens to captain it. Oh, that's the yacht Al Masih presented to Blackstone a couple of years ago, and Art Blackstone renamed it *Obsidian*. Al Masih presented Blackstone both yacht and captain when he replaced it with a newer, better version."

"Means Jeffrys is a plank owner of that yacht," observed Orbison.

"What does that mean, Chief?" asked Larry.

"Son," Orbison said, "in the navy, when a boat's captain is with the boat from drawin' board through shakedown, launch and all of its service, he is said to own a plank of the boat's deck. No one will know that boat better."

"So, if Jeffrys says there are no bad guys hiding out on it, he should know, right?"

"Right, Stringbean. That is exactly what it means."

The rest of the names on the list of household staff were all American born, and the background checks revealed nothing to raise red flags. Aims sat staring into space for a few moments, silently.

Rick noticed and finally spoke.

"What do you think, Aims? You're quiet."

"In Baton Rouge," she began, "when my momma was planning a party or big event, she would hire a party planner. They were a team of a planners who arranged decorators, caterers, waitstaff, and cleanup. All temporary staff were employed by the planner, but they had the run of the house before, during, and after the event. The planner issued keys and authorization IDs and was responsible for returning all that when the contract ended. Larry, let's look at White's list again, can we, please? I don't recall seeing the name of any temporary contractors on it."

When their search yielded nothing, Aims pulled her notepad out.

"What are you doing, Aims?" Rick asked.

"Starting a list of questions I want to ask the Blackstones. Let's call our friends in the US marshals' office to get a federal warrant to search White's quarters. We can serve it and execute it when we go there."

"If the marshals get the warrant for us, we'll have to take them with us to execute it. You know, *quid pro quo*," Rick said.

"What would we be lookin' for?" Orbison asked.

"I'm not sure. Maybe a notation of a contact of his personally, which he did not put on the list he gave us. I'd just like to see what's in White's quarters at the Marco Island estate."

"Maybe we should check with the marshals and see if they have any questions about what would be there. That way, we'd be on the plus side of the equation by offering an in to the estate," Larry said.

"I'll call one of the guys who was questioning White and the others," Rick said. "Let's see what we can come up with. We can proceed from there." He pulled out his cell phone to make the call. Before he could begin to make the connection, the Skype program beeped on the plasma.

The team gathered around Larry's laptop as he connected the call. Secretary of the Navy Admiral Johnson's face came up on one side of the split screen, and Severin Collier's face was showing on the other side.

"Hello, team," SECNAV said. "How are you all?"

"Just preparing to secure a federal search warrant for White's quarters at the Blackstone estate, sir," Rick replied.

"I need you to belay that order, for the moment," Johnson said. "Why is that?"

"Well, the short version is I blinked first."

"Beg your pardon, sir?"

"I just got off a conference call between the secretary of defense, the attorney general, and myself, and when they put me on the spot about the status of your investigation, I blinked first."

"What exactly does that mean, sir?" Aims asked.

"It means that this investigation enters a different phase. On the one hand, there is the investigation into the federal crimes committed by those who brought down Blackstone's plane."

"You mean their assault on federal officers," Rick said,

"interfering with a federal investigation, domestic terrorist activities, and the attempt to take over an American corporation in order to secure American technology for a foreign power?"

"Yes," Johnson replied. "All of that. Department of Justice wants all of the information you have gathered that pertains to those crimes to be turned over to the US marshals so that they can build their cases against the suspects they are now holding in custody."

"The other phase," inserted Collier, "pertains to the investigation of the plane crash itself, and NTSB will need your input to document and collate the evidence we now have in our hangar here in Brunswick, as well as the last bits and pieces that your investigation there has uncovered."

"In other words," Larry said. "Wrap it up and return to base. Right, sir?"

"Essentially, yes," Johnson said. "I know you'll have to make another contact with Blackstone, to inform him of this change, and you'll need another meeting with the marshals to hand off evidence and bring them up to speed on what you've been doing, but, Robb, you're right."

"You're going to be busy for some time, pulling everything together with the NTSB," Collier said. "They have been complaining that they were missing key information in the compilation of data for their report, and how much they needed the firsthand statements to fill in those gaps. So don't think this is over yet. There is still a lot to be done before any findings can be reported to anyone."

"I'm thinking," Rick said, "that we need to make a copy of the information on the flash drive that Art Blackstone gave us on the Onyx Group. A sort of insurance policy. What do you think about that, boss?"

"Couldn't hurt," Collier said. "Could it, sir?" he asked Johnson.

"What is your saying, Chief?" Johnson said, addressing Orbison for the first time in the conversation.

"Better to have it and not need it, sir," Orbison said, chuckling, "than need it and not have it."

"Yeah." Johnson smiled. "That's the one."

"Okay, sirs," Rick said to their two superiors. "We'll take care of the loose ends here and let you know our ETA in Brunswick."

Aims grimaced. No chance for her and Rick to talk. *Guess it will have to wait.*

Chapter 14

Aims turned away from the huge three-dimensional jigsaw puzzle she, her team, and the National Traffic Safety Board investigators had been working on. It had been a long day. In fact, it had been a long week.

It had taken a couple of days to get clear from Naples. When she and the team had arrived back in Brunswick from Naples, Florida, and they walked into the hangar, she felt a flash of recognition. It looked like a partially assembled airplane made from an Erector set, but the child assembling it had gotten tired of the task and walked away, leaving pieces and parts scattered across the floor. These past few days had been spent sorting and finding tab A to insert into slot B.

What now lay on the floor of the giant hangar was a nearly reassembled aircraft. On the work benches sat the fluorescent orange plastic components, usually referred to as black boxes, and their circuit boards sprouted connector wires to adjacent computers, although the computers were now shut down for the evening. Aims and Rick were the last ones to depart. Rick had been helping Larry and the NTSB people with the reassembly of the wreckage into a recognizable aircraft again, in order to assess exactly what had been destroyed by the missile. Aims had been sorting through computer files for the last several hours, in order to establish a timeline for the involvement of Al Masih's family with the Onyx Group in general and to discover the degree of involvement with the crash of the plane and the deaths of the two naval officers.

As Aims dismounted from the high stool at the work station, Rick emerged from the employee lounge area, drying his hands on a clean grease rag.

"Oh, good. You're still here. I was hoping you would be," he said.

"Oh, yeah?" Aims said. "Were you scared to be alone in the dark?"

"Could be." Rick grinned. "Can't think of anyone I'd rather be alone in the dark with than you. You keep a stiletto in your boot. Tends to make me feel safer."

"You seem to have forgotten I'm the one who got taken for a ride in the dark not so long ago. The stiletto was no help. If you hadn't come to my rescue, I am afraid to speculate on what would have happened."

"Well, maybe we should think about staying close so we can keep each other safe," Rick said.

"Is that why you're glad I'm still here?"

"Oh, I'm always glad you're here. But I've been working on a craving for pizza for the last hour, and I don't think I can eat a whole one by myself. But I'm not in the mood to take home leftovers. Or at least I'd like to get someone else to take home leftovers too."

"So, your misery wants company? Is that it?"

Rick was grinning widely as he nodded.

"Okay," Aims said. "But you have to pick up half the tab."

"Hey," he said. "If you go with me, I'll take the whole tab. My uncle raised me right."

"Deal. Just let me shut down this computer and freshen up a bit. Be back in five."

Aims waited at the table while Rick placed their order at the window. This pizzeria was a favorite of the office staff, and Aims trusted Rick to remember that she didn't want anchovies. In a few moments, he set their large iced teas on the table along with the numbered placard identifying their order. The place was pleasantly crowded with a fairly high ambient noise level, but their booth at the back corner gave them a sense of privacy.

"Funny how we seem to end up here after a tough field trip," Aims said. "Do you think we're in a rut?"

"Nah," Rick said. "We just have some comfortable routines."

"That does sound better."

The server brought their order to the table, two extra-large pizzas on pedestal trays, each with different toppings.

"You weren't kidding about taking home leftovers, were you?" Aims said. "Although I find that I'm hungrier than I thought, and the smell is tantalizing.

"And speaking of tantalizing," she continued. "Did you know that the rare metal for which Al Masih wanted Art Blackstone's extraction method is named for the Greek god, Tantalus?"

"Isn't he the one who stole food from the banquet table of the gods and was sentenced to eternally stand in a pool of water, the branches of a fruit tree just out of reach overhead, and the waters of the pool below out of reach for him to drink? Hence the term tantalize?"

"That's the one. I've been going through the information that Blackstone gave us on that flash drive. He's a good researcher. He included that little tidbit from Greek mythology as well as describing how he got hooked up with Al Masih."

"I get the feeling he's pretty good at whatever he undertakes," Rick commented. "How did he get involved with the Arab nabob?"

"I was intrigued by that whole narrative," Aims said, reaching for another slice of pizza.

"Remember how I told you about getting hooked on aviation after a visit to a local airfield with a college friend?"

"Yeah, I remember. At the time, your dad said he was sure your whole life had become derailed by that little momentary obsession, as he called it."

"Sometimes the most innocent accidental encounter like that can shape a person's whole life," Aims said. "Art Blackstone's university major was metallurgy, and as a part of that study, he had to take a course in rare metals. One of the metals he studied was tantalum, and when he went back to the Port of Miami for his summer job, he encountered the reclamation operation of extracting tantalum from scrapped electronic and surgical instruments. Because getting the ore was so difficult, the remanufacture of it into newer, better products really paid off. Blackstone decided to see if he could improve on the remanufacturing process on one hand and simplify the mining process on the other hand. You could say Blackstone was tantalized by tantalum."

"Bad pun, Aims," Rick said. "But accurate nonetheless. How did Al Masih get into the picture?"

"Remember," Aims said, "the fourth largest naturally occurring deposit of tantalum lies in the northwest corner of Arabia. Seems that the tribal council in the kingdom is made up of the most influential princes of the royal family, and some of them are responsible for most of the aspects of daily life of the populace in specific areas. Al Masih is the prince who has control of that northwest area of the kingdom, and he has made improving the economy and living conditions of the people living in his area a major project."

"Didn't I read somewhere that Arab oil reserves will run out in the foreseeable future?" Rick asked.

"Yes, you did," Aims answered. "That is why Al Masih is anxious to find some resource that he has access to and control of, to replace the oil when it runs out. Not only will that accomplish his purpose in his area of influence, but it will also make him a major player on the tribal council.

"Blackstone managed to arrange a field trip to Arabia to see the geologic deposits of tantalum, *in situ*, and while he was there, he got noticed by the prince."

"In other words," Rick said, pushing back his plate and wiping his mouth and hands, "Al Masih recognized a kindred hungry spirit in Blackstone and decided to see if he could exploit the naïve, ugly American."

"Yeah," Aims replied. "But Al Masih's xenophobia blinded him to Blackstone's ability to recognize a predator when he saw one. So, he let Al Masih become an investor of Onyx Group but made very sure that the degree of influence that he wielded in the corporation was carefully limited. That is where Alexa and her family come into the mix.

"While their relationship is really a love match, Alexa considers herself an equal partner with Art, and her family is overflowing with attorneys specializing in commercial law. In their world, foreign investors were the bane of their existence, and they were happy to provide contract wording that would protect Alexa and her husband from predatory foreign investors. A tenet of their operation was that Middle Eastern investors were certain to be after *something*, and they were determined that there would be nothing left on the table for Al Masih. They provided the Blackstones with this caveat in a cover letter on the first contract that they provided and that Art Blackstone and Al Masih signed together. Al Masih never expected that level of knowledge and sophistication from either Art or Alexa. So he did not pay a lot of attention to the fine print in the contracts he signed, and consequently, he was not aware of the extent of control being exercised over his involvement."

"What did all this have to do with the deaths of our two naval officers?"

"That," said Aims, "was a monumental miscalculation on the part of Al Masih, White, and Al Masih's two sons."

"How so?"

"Well, the twins enrolled in MIT, majoring in microelectronics, for both their undergraduate and graduate degrees. Their joint master's thesis was titled 'Remote Access of Targeted Munitions in Order to Correct Glitches in Input.' Their paper included innovations to the overall design of the chips, and Al Masih showed it to Art Blackstone as an offered design for a new product."

"Why would Art accept the design of a new product with a built-in access point to change its target in midflight?" Rick asked. "That seems to go against everything we've learned about Art Blackstone so far."

"Well," Aims replied, "seems that Art learned a thing or two from his in-laws. He made copies of the original design he had approved. That design did not have that backdoor feature. His contract with the Al Masih twins specified that any design changes from the original would require negotiation of a new contract. All the signees of that contract agreed to those conditions and stipulations."

"So, what happened?"

"This is the point where White inserts himself into the operation. When the twins submitted the design changes, White intercepted them at the beginning of the approval process and signed Art Blackstone's name to amendment documents to the approved design and the contract modification. He claimed he was acting with Blackstone's authorization, but these signatures were illegal, or at least unauthorized. I think this is the opening move to what ultimately led to the deaths of Admiral Carter, Captain Wilford, and pilot Joe Grimes. Every subsequent move was made to cover up this irregularity in the manufacture and distribution of the chips."

"Wow," Rick said. "Looks like Art Blackstone hit pay dirt when he went digging in Onyx Group records. All of this information was on that flash drive?"

"It was."

"I'm sort of glad we made a copy of it before turning it over to the marshals. It answers a lot of question, as it pertains to the prosecution of federal crimes but also as it pertains to the actual crash of Art's plane.

"Speaking of which," he continued, "what are the forensic findings concerning the deaths of those on the plane?"

"Well, our ME says that both the pilot, Admiral Carter, and Wilford were all shot with the same weapon."

"In other words," Rick said, "the three bullets were shot by the same gun and show identical ballistics."

"Right," Aims replied. "And the time of death for each victim is within sixty minutes of each other. Wilford's body indicates that it was submerged postmortem. I think we can say, from the evidence, that Wilford was met when he parachuted to earth out of the plane, which was almost certainly immediately prior to the missile hit, and the Admiral's briefcase, which he had with him, was handed over to those who met him. We know that White himself was not part of that welcoming committee, but it is certain that it was arranged by him. After they relieved Wilford of the briefcase, they took the weapon he had used on the plane and killed him with it. Then they cut away the shroud lines from his parachute and weighted his body before tossing it into the water and making their escape. Finding the murder weapon itself and fingering the mastermind of the operation will be the task of the federal prosecutor."

"From what I saw," Rick said, "of the motley crew that White had working for him, getting one or all of them to roll over on White might take a little time and some plea offers, but overall, I think they will turn out to be pretty weak links in the chain."

"I think you're right."

"What about Wilford's shooting of the admiral and the pilot?" Rick asked. "What will happen about that?"

"I'm not sure," Aims said. "Seems a little pointless to pursue any charges posthumously. After all, Wilford comes from a navy family. They'll understand about a funeral without full military honors. I think that they, SECNAV, and DOJ will work something out that should be satisfactory to all parties concerned."

"That flash drive was chock-full of information," Rick observed. "Glad we copied it before giving it away to the marshals."

"Speaking of being chock-full," Aims said, "I think I've eaten as much pizza as I can this evening. Let's ask the server for boxes for your leftovers."

"Yours too. We'll need two boxes. I assume you know that the most nutritious breakfast is cold pizza. We've got to stay healthy in order to wrap this up," Rick said.

While they waited for their carry-out cartons, Rick eyed Aims thoughtfully. "How much more work is left on this report by us and the NTSB?"

"Just putting it all down in a document," Aims replied. "When they left this afternoon, the NTSB people said tomorrow would probably be a short day. They plan to email all the supporting documents and their narrative to their office staff at home for compilation and distribution. We and SECNAV will get our copies, and after a proofread and we indicate our concurrence, it will be published.

"So, as I said, a short day tomorrow. How much more work has to be done on the reconstruction of the wreckage? They will probably need to take detailed photos to document the exact damage done to the aircraft by the missile."

"I think we're done except for picking up tools and scraps," Rick said. "The guys I've been working with said to look my best tomorrow. Tomorrow is picture day."

As they were walking out of the pizzeria, their phones chirped in unison. When they checked them, they each found a text message from Collier, asking them to meet him in his office at the beginning of their day tomorrow.

Aims slid the carton of leftover pizza into her sparsely populated refrigerator. A wilted stalk of celery and a single egg seemed to be waiting for some company.

Got to get some groceries when I get done tomorrow. Good thing Rick invited me to have pizza with him. I could have starved without it. Wonder if we'll get to have our talk soon.

As she climbed into bed, she thought of her promise to herself that night at the Coast Guard station in Fort Meyers Beach after her rescue. Her mind ran through the conversation with Rick at the pizzeria, as it had all the way home from the restaurant. No, she had been right not to bring up her feelings for Rick tonight. It was important to them both that when they discussed their relationship, their minds were ready to focus on that and nothing else. That could not happen until their investigation was safely put to rest. *But soon, Lord. Please?*

❧ ⟞⟐⟝ ❧

When Rick opened his refrigerator to deposit the leftover pizza, it too looked quite barren. A couple of bottles of water sat chilling on the top shelf. Mustard and ketchup sat forlornly on the shelf of the door. The icemaker bucket was full, but the automatic cut-off when the bucket was full had functioned per design, and it had not overflowed while he ignored it. The pizza box held the only real food, and he knew his pantry was similarly depleted.

He mentally started a to-do list, and restocking was the first item.

He stared into his eyes in the mirror over the sink in his bathroom as he brushed his teeth in preparation for bed. He wondered if Aims had reviewed their conversation that evening, as he had. Several times that evening, he had remembered his need to let her know that he wanted her to be a permanent part of his life. But it had not felt right, so he had set the thought aside. Instead of fretting about it, however, he felt at peace. *When the time is right, that's when.*

When they entered their boss's office the following morning, he motioned them to seats.

"Where are we, Rick?"

"Well, boss," he said, "according to the NTSB people, today is wrap day. They are taking pictures of the reassembled wreckage, and the analysts working with Aims are emailing their data and support documents, along with a narrative, to their home office to be compiled and forwarded to us for concurrence. Once they get that, they will publish it with copies to us and SECNAV. So when they finish with us, and they said it would be a short day today, we'll be done with this assignment."

"SECNAV wants me to tell you that he's putting letters of commendation for a job well done in your files and Agent Robb's. He also suggested that you might want a week's paid leave as a bonus for the intense time in south Florida. Of course," he added, "we'll need to have your itinerary and contact information in case something comes up while you're off."

"In other words," Aims said with a smile, "we have a week off but with a short leash."

"Isn't that usually the case?" Collier said with a nod.

"That's been my experience in the navy," Aims said.

"The Marine Corps wasn't much different," Rick added.

Chapter 15

The wrap-up of the investigation was a little more complicated than simply waving goodbye to the visiting NTSB analysts, but finally Rick, Larry, and Aims were able to head home, released from duty for a week's paid leave. Aims had registered with Collier's office, leaving her cell phone number as a point of contact and an itinerary tagged with the notation that it would be announced later.

Aims had just pushed her front door closed with her foot, her hands full of grocery bags, when her cell phone chirped. She hurriedly emptied her hands and checked the incoming call. Rick.

"Hey, Rick."

"What are you doing right now?"

"I stopped at the supermarket on my way home. You?"

"Me too. But when I walked in, I realized that I missed being with you and wondered if you'd keep me company this evening."

"What did you have in mind?"

"Well, you know how I moved into this apartment about a week before we got the call out for the plane crash in Naples?"

"Yeah," Aims said. "As I recall, you just finished emptying boxes the night before we left."

"That's right. One of the features of this high-rise condo complex is that every apartment has a deep, private balcony and a built-in gas grill that is connected to the building's natural gas line. I wanted to try it out, but after the pleasant grilling sessions with Chief Orbison, it felt sort of empty to do it alone. How about you come over and we'll christen it together. I brought home some chicken and some basic salad greens. Want to bring some dressing for the salad?"

"Sure. Anything else I can bring?"

"Beside yourself? Whatever you think. I have bread, vegetable skewers, and sorbet. And of course iced tea and one of those one-cup coffee brewers with a whole rack of flavored blends."

"Sounds wonderful. Text me the address. I'll put away my groceries and change into civvies. How long should it take me to drive there?"

"It's about the same time as going from your place to the field office. I'm sending you the address now."

"Okay. See you in about three-quarters of an hour."

Aims programmed the address into her navigation system as she drove away from her apartment. She loved the drive through Brunswick, because there was still a feel of a small town, in spite of the growing size of the city. Believing that Rick's new place would be in the same general area where he had lived before, she was surprised that the instructions led her away from the riverfront complex and sent her toward the causeway and the high-rise condominium complex on Saint Simon Island. In the years they had worked together at the Brunswick office, Rick lived on a converted river barge that he and his uncles had constructed. It was a lovely mixture of sleek modern and rustic and was utterly charming. Rick had hosted the office Christmas party there a couple of years ago, and it was a delightful experience for everyone. It was perfectly situated in the area of Brunswick that the chamber of commerce liked to tout as a piece of Natchez under the hill. It was a blend of blatant riverfront dives, fast-food places, pawnshops, and elegant dining places.

Now she was directed toward a district that bristled with high-rise condominium towers that were clearly designed to exude luxury and opulence. The drastic difference between that setting of waterway living and this setting was going to take some getting used to. *This can't be right. Maybe I entered the address wrong. Let me check Rick's text message again. Here it is. Nope. I entered it right. Could the navigation system have a glitch? Possibly, but I don't think so. I'll give it a little time. If I don't find the address soon, I'll call Rick and verify that I'm in the right neighborhood.*

Having settled on that contingency plan, she kept driving. She was sent across the causeway and onto the Saint Simon Island area to where the condos had views of the Brunswick River on one side and the Atlantic Ocean on the other. She made the turn into a short cul-de-sac and was immediately confronted with a gate house occupied by two uniformed attendants.

She pulled up and lowered her window.

"Good afternoon, ma'am. How can we help you?"

What is this? Gatekeeper and valet? Where am I anyway? Maybe I fell down a rabbit hole like Alice.

"Uh, I'm here to see Rick Holt. Am I in the right place?"

"Yes, ma'am. He recently joined us as the new owner of unit 15 A. Could you give me your name please? And I need to just glance at your identification, if it is not too much trouble."

"My name is Amelia Wallace," she said, handing him her federal credentials.

He glanced at his computer monitor and then nodded his head toward his companion.

"If you'll leave your keys in the car and take whatever you'll need while you're here, we'll park for you and call Mr. Holt with your ticket number. Do you need assistance in carrying anything?"

Wow. That will take a moment to digest. Okay. I can do this.

"No, thank you. I just have one bag. It's not heavy, and I can handle it."

Aims turned off the ignition, picked up the bag she had packed with additions to their dinner, and got out of the car. The uniformed valet held out his hand to assist her. After thanking him, she walked the short distance to the portico of the building. A uniformed doorman held the door for her and directed her to the elevators. She was standing in a sleek, modern atrium, replete with potted plants, walls of glass, and a desk. Behind the desk was a uniformed security guard, seated beside a bank of monitors, showing various views where surveillance cameras were operating. Her glance took in the pool view, parking garage, gated entrance she just passed through, and the service entrance with loading dock and trash receptacles. She didn't have time to catch all of the views before the elevator door opened, accompanied by a soft chime.

Her gaze swept over the view from the glass-enclosed elevator car as it rose up the side of the tower. As she looked around the foyer that the elevator opened to, she saw only two apartments on that level. How had Rick managed such a huge uptick in lifestyle? Maybe she could get him to tell her before the evening was over.

Rick was standing before the door marked 15 A. She set down

her tote bag and framed his face with both her hands. With a mock-serious expression, she turned his face from side to side, as if examining an unfamiliar piece of sculpture. Rick submitted silently to her shenanigans, knowing that when she spoke, it would probably set the tone for their whole evening.

Finally she released him and picked up her belongings.

"Yup," she said. "Right guy. Don't recognize any of the rest of this at all."

Rick wrapped his arms around her in a smothering embrace before taking her bag of goodies and leading her into the apartment.

As he set the tote bag on the counter in the kitchen, he turned and said, "You like?"

"Well, yeah. I guess," she said. "But it is so different from your last residence. What happened?"

"One of my buddies in the Marine Corps came to visit me a year or so ago, and I gave him a tour of my house barge. He was very intrigued with it and how well it would accommodate his family. Two of his children are in primary classes, and he and his wife were considering homeschooling them. Their youngest is just walking. Both their families are involved in a successful interstate architecture firm, and Mike, my buddy, does the fieldwork, which includes preliminary investigation, soil samples, and geological considerations. Their main area of operation is along the Mississippi, Missouri, and Tennessee River valleys, and Mike has had to be away from home a lot. They thought about moving their family into an RV so they could spend the time he has to be in the field with him, but they were unhappy about the restrictiveness of such a move. He met one of my uncles on a trip, and my uncle told Mike about our house barge and said he should visit mine to give him an idea what we could do.

"He spent a couple of days taking pictures and looking at the designs and specs before he went back to his family. They convened a meeting of his family and all the in-laws, all of them officers of the family corporation, and the upshot of it all was, as they say, an offer I could not refuse. This condo tower is one of Mike's family's first projects, and in addition to a generous offer for the barge, they gave me a great deal on this place."

"And the reason for their generosity was …?" Aims asked.

"When we were in Afghanistan," Rick said, "Mike's platoon was escorting a convoy of some UN peacekeepers along a back road. Mike was riding in the lead-armored personnel carrier when it hit a roadside IED, and the platoon and convoy were pinned down and taking hostile fire. The marines had me on roving assignment, tasked to do overwatch and protection for such excursions. I had been waiting in the rocks overlooking that road for three days before they came into view. I already located the enemy emplacement, and as soon as the APC went up, I began firing silenced sniper rounds as covering fire. At the same time, I called for backup and rescue. Several of Mike's men didn't make it, but Mike was fortunate and only left the lower half of one leg behind. The rehab team was as awesome for him as they were for you, and Mike can still dance with his wife and race his kids."

"Wow," Aims said. "What an amazing story. That makes this place even more impressive."

"How about a guided tour?" Rick asked. "Dinner can wait."

"I'd love it. How much room do you have?"

"I have three bedrooms, each with its own bath, en suite, plus the master." The décor was sort of sterile and modern, and she did not recognize any of the furnishings. But then he'd only been there a couple of weeks. He'd probably be making some significant changes.

He led her farther into the apartment, where she found a spacious, open living space and a dining area open to the kitchen. He led her through the kitchen and through some glazed French doors onto the balcony. "Here is where I've already begun to take my morning coffee and evening meals," he said as they stepped out onto a deep and shaded private area that offered Aims views of the Brunswick River and cityscape on one hand and a generous slice of the Atlantic Ocean on the other. The side next to the building contained a full outdoor kitchen, complete with granite counters surrounding the natural gas grill, food prep station with a sink, and cabinetry for storage. Chicken breasts, salad greens, and a wooden salad bowl and tongs lay ready for use.

"The condo comes with maintenance, maid service, and the valet parking you already encountered. There is a twenty-four hour doorman with security on-site and gardeners and pool service, all paid for by the homeowners' association annual fees. We also have a secured parking garage for two cars with storage area.

"So, Aims, why don't we see what you brought with you, and we'll continue our meal preparation?"

"Good idea," she said. "I'm beginning to get hungry. In spite of being in awe of your new digs."

As they stepped back into the kitchen, Aims became aware of the soft, subtle strains of music. "What are we listening to?" she asked.

"I'm a fan of seventies' folk and gospel classics from the same period. If you don't like it, I can change it."

"No," she said. "I like it. It's soothing." She began removing items from her tote bag. Rick fixed her a large glass of iced tea and carried it and dinnerware out to the table on the balcony. She had brought raspberry vinaigrette dressing along with strawberries, walnuts, and cherry tomatoes to add to the salad greens at the food prep station outside. She caught a whiff of garlic as she began to create the salad in the wooden bowl. Rick began marinating the chicken before they settled into seats at the table to watch the sky over the ocean darken into deep twilight as the first stars appeared.

"I've been concerned about you, Aims." Rick finally broke the comfortable silence.

"How so?" she asked.

"Well, you took quite a beating from White and his cohorts before we could get to you, and you've hardly had time to recuperate. We've been so busy wrapping things up. How are you? And don't brush off my question. I want to know how you *really* are."

"I'm better than I ever thought I could be," she replied.

"What made the difference?" he asked. "Larry and I were going to loosen the tie-downs of that chopper. It had not even registered that they were already undone when I heard the door of the cabin slam shut, the rotors wind up, and the chopper fly off, practically out of our hands. I watched it pass overhead in the dark, and I thought I had lost you for good. It felt like looking into an abyss. I never want to feel that way again."

The emotion in his voice touched some deep place in Aims that she had not known was there. For a moment, she could not make her voice work.

"What made the difference?" she asked when her voice worked again. "The difference was I prayed. Like I seldom have before. I began to understand what you and my parents have been telling me.

I realized that I had no control over what was happening. That I never have had any real control over what has happened in my life. That it was time for me to take my hands off the controls and let the Lord take over, without any more interference from me. I confessed that I knew I didn't deserve any of His help but that I needed it. That whatever help He gave would be enough, and I would be grateful. That is the difference. When I let go of it all, I was at peace, and believe it or not, I fell asleep. Really asleep and not just unconscious.

"Remember when they got me back to the Coast Guard station, and the doctors did an MRI of my brain? They said there was no evidence of any swelling or concussion. You heard them tell me that. They were amazed. And me? I was grateful.

"When I prayed, I told the Lord I would give Him credit for His deliverance, regardless of what method He used. Even if it was by sending you. And I do give Him credit, and I thank Him. And you for being His method of deliverance."

The silence that stretched between them was not uncomfortable but felt right.

After a while, the timer chimed, and they both roused to finish the preparation of their dinner. Rick put the chicken and vegetable skewers on the grill, and Aims refilled their glasses of tea. They worked as a team placing condiments and seasonings on the table, and then Rick plated their meal, and they were seated again.

Rick reached out a hand to Aims, and she took it. They bowed their heads, and Rick's prayer was only three words. "Thank you, Lord." They were busy with their meal and spoke very little until Rick cleared their empty plates.

"Come choose your favorite blend of coffee, Aims," he said. "I'll get our sorbet from the freezer."

When they were seated again, Aims again reached out to Rick.

"You said that when you thought I was gone for good, that it was like looking into an abyss. I recognize that kind of feeling. One of the things I had to let go of was the thought of never having the chance to let you know how I feel about you. But when I was delivered, I asked for the chance to tell you that, since I was still alive. I think now is the time."

"I agree," Rick said.

"I know you've worked for my dad for several years and that you're acquainted with my parents." At Rick's nod, she continued. "You've heard from them about my growing-up years."

Again, Rick nodded. "What you haven't heard, because I have never said it to anyone, is how I felt about things during that growing-up process." Rick waited out the ensuing pause without speaking.

"My parents were a sharp contrast. On the one hand, my mom was raised as a southern debutante from a well-to-do family. Dad too, but along with that, he had a fierce hunger to become a success in the state attorney's office—*to show his family* was how he put it. In retrospect, I guess he battled an inferiority complex, and so have I. My dad could even have caused it. Along with that, Dad was very controlling. My mother accepted and encouraged his dictates. So our family life was a strange mixture of affluence and strict puritanism.

"I know you've discovered that I can never resist a challenge, and Dad's efforts to dictate my choices were something I could neither ignore nor agree to. So my efforts to chart my own course led me to Annapolis with a full-ride scholarship. Because the legal profession was what I knew best, I aimed for JAG."

Rick's hand motion invited her to continue.

"A chance friendship and visit to a local flying school, along with a plane ride, hooked me on flying. The scholarship committee let me trade my commitment to JAG for an active enlistment in the navy with flight school thrown in.

"Praying at meals and bedtimes were an inescapable part of my life. But I realize now that the idea of divine guidance was a concept I never fully understood. It seemed a lot like what I grew up with. With Dad."

Rick laughed. "I don't think I've ever heard anyone describe it so well," he said. "It is a tough concept to grasp, and I think a lot of kids raised in devout Christian homes struggle with it. I know I did."

"You did? I never knew that."

"I think this is going to be an interesting conversation," he said.

"Anyway, you know about the posting to a fighter squadron in the Med and the crash during a night landing."

His nod encouraged her to continue.

"When I lost visibility of the ball for landing, I began to pray. I was desperate not to crash. The lack of visibility and the motion of the carrier deck made my undercarriage catch on the edge of the flight deck. The rest was a foregone conclusion."

"And so was your conclusion that God had forsaken you," Rick commented.

"Yeah. You got that."

"You know, Aims," he said. "So did God."

"What do you mean?"

"His love for His children is unconditional. That's why He says He has us tattooed on His palms. So that we know He'll never forget us. And He not only sees what we do, but He knows why we do it."

"That's what you meant when you said He had not forsaken

me, or I wouldn't have recovered as totally as I did." At his nod, she went on.

"Over the years, watching you and learning about your faith, I've learned some of that for myself. I've also realized that your friendship and support are also evidence that He has not forsaken me. The more you talked about God's love, and the more you demonstrated it in your life, the more I began to understand and hunger for that for myself. Hearing you talk to Him like a good and personal friend shone a new light on things. I've come to the conclusion that bringing you into my life was God's answer to my prayer when I was fighting to land my plane. I don't know what benefit is yours, being in my life, but I am thankful for you with almost every breath I take. I realize that I love you. I want you to be a part of my life. I want to be a part of yours."

Rick's silence was so long that Aims fought the inner urge to panic. Finally, he reached out and took her hand.

"Now, it is my turn to share with you what I've told no one else." The light pressure of Aims's hand seemed to encourage him.

"My mom was a single parent, living near the waterfront in Baton Rouge. She struggled to take care of my brother and me, but she had few skills to qualify her for a good-paying job. She refused to take any help from her brothers, choosing to work two jobs. No one ever told me what those two jobs were. My brother was older, but he and I learned to take care of each other while Mom was gone for hours at a time. We became each other's best friend, promising to always have each other's back.

"Then, one night, one of my uncles came and got my brother and me and took us home with him. The next day, we learned that Mom had been the victim of a war between rival drug dealers, and she was shot during the showdown. A few months later, my brother found one of my uncle's guns and decided to avenge my mom's death. All he succeeded in doing was getting himself killed, and I felt like I'd lost a part of myself.

"I never felt like I'd found that missing part, until I found you in that hospital room in Bethesda. You have that same spunky spirit that my brother, Derek, had. With you, I feel like we can take on the world—do anything. Make things right. Solve problems. Take care of people. I feel like I've found my best friend. Like you're the other part of me."

Still holding her hand, he slid out of his chair and knelt beside hers.

"I love you, Aims Wallace. I want you in my life. Walk with me. Talk to me. Live with me. Marry me. Grow old with me. Let us see what life together can become."

Aims felt the tears begin to fall as she saw the emotion in his eyes. Then she found herself on her knees, facing him. Their arms encircled each other.

"Welcome home, Aims," Rick said.

"Welcome home, Rick," she said as their lips met.

Dear Reader,

It took years to know Aims and Rick. During those years, I experienced the pain of having my worst fears come to pass, even as I prayed they would not. This is when I had to learn that God meant what He said: "I will not forget you. You are tattooed on My palm."

His faithfulness in answering the prayers I could not pray and sending people into my life at just the right time brought me to a new place of blessing and love. Just like He did for Aims and Rick.

Thank you for taking the time to read Aims and Rick's story. I hope you enjoyed it and are encouraged to keep trusting the one who loves you so much He tattoos your name on His palm.

I would love to hear about your journey. You can reach me via email at nlcarter22@yahoo.com.

About the Author

Naomi L. Carter has written short articles for newspapers since the 1980s. She is the author of a self-published novel, *in DANGER*, an inspirational suspense romance. Naomi is a member of the Central Florida chapter of American Christian Fiction Writers and has a master's degree in counseling and guidance from Liberty University. She was a registered individual and family counselor in Washington State for twenty years. In 2012, Naomi reconnected with her high school sweetheart, following fifty-eight years of separation. They consider themselves newlyweds.